"I was being followed," she fabricated, "by this really creepy guy. I saw you sitting in here all alone, and I thought maybe you wouldn't mind helping me out by pretending to be, you know, my significant other or something, so this guy will leave me alone once and for all . . . ?"

He looked out the window into the crowded street. "Is he still out there?"

Maggie turned to look. "I . . . don't know." She hated lying like this. She was amazed that she could come up with a story so quickly with those disturbing brown eyes gazing at her. But there was no way she could tell him the truth.

"Well, just in case he's still watching . . ." Charles leaned forward and kissed her.

He kissed her.

On the mouth.

His lips were warm and soft and he tasted like lemonade.

Maggie was caught so off guard, she could do nothing but laugh.

He laughed too.

"Maybe we better do that again," he suggested, his grin widening. "Make sure this man—whoever he is—really gets the message."

And then he was kissing her again. Not a swift gentle brushing of lips like the last kiss, but a longer, deeper kiss. Maggie felt a jolt of disbelief as his tongue swept into her mouth. Not disbelief that he would kiss her that way, but that she would welcome such a kiss, that she would kiss him back with such abandon, and most of all, that she wanted that kiss to go on and on and on.

WHAT ARE *LOVESWEPT* ROMANCES?

They are stories of true romance and touching emotion. We believe those two very important ingredients are constants in our highly sensual and very believable stories in the LOVE-SWEPT line. Our goal is to give you, the reader, stories of consistently high quality that may sometimes make you laugh, sometimes make you cry, but are always fresh and creative and contain many delightful surprises within their pages.

Most romance fans read an enormous number of books. Those they truly love, they keep. Others may be traded with friends and soon forgotten. We hope that each LOVESWEPT romance will be a treasure—a "keeper." We will always try to publish

LOVE STORIES YOU'LL NEVER FORGET
BY AUTHORS YOU'LL ALWAYS REMEMBER

The Editors

TIME ENOUGH FOR LOVE

SUZANNE BROCKMANN

BANTAM BOOKS
NEW YORK · TORONTO · LONDON · SYDNEY · AUCKLAND

TIME ENOUGH FOR LOVE
A Bantam Book / November 1997

ISBN 0-553-44597-9

Published simultaneously in the United States and Canada

Bantam Books are published by Bantam Books, a division of Bantam
Doubleday Dell Publishing Group, Inc. Its trademark, consisting of the
words "Bantam Books" and the portrayal of a rooster, is Registered in U.S.
Patent and Trademark Office and in other countries. Marca Registrada.
Bantam Books, 1540 Broadway, New York, New York 10036.

PRINTED IN THE UNITED STATES OF AMERICA
OPM   10 9 8 7 6 5 4 3 2 1

For my Gram & Gramps, Fred and Tilly Brockmann, on their 68th wedding anniversary, with all my love.

ONE

There was a naked man pounding on Maggie Winthrop's back door.

She did a double take as she looked out her kitchen window and realized that he was covered with dirt, as if he'd been crawling around in her garden. Dirt and . . . could that possibly be blood? Streaks of something that looked like blood were on his shoulder and arm. He was wild-eyed, with dark, shaggy hair that exploded around his face, looking as if he'd just been ejected from a wind tunnel.

And yes, he was definitely, undeniably naked.

Somehow he knew her name. "Maggie!" he shouted, hammering on the door. "Mags, let me in!"

It was locked, thank God, and Maggie ran to be sure the front door was locked as well.

She had her cordless phone in her hand, ready to call the police when he called out again.

"Maggie! God, please be home!" There was such anguish in the man's voice. Anguish and something that

1

stopped her from dialing the phone. Something oddly familiar.

Maggie took the stairs to the second floor of her house two at a time. She set the phone down on the vanity of the sink as she used both hands to open the bathroom window and push up the screen.

The man heard the noise, and he stopped pounding on the door. He looked up at her expectantly as she peered down at him.

"Maggie." There was such relief in the way he said her name. But despite the strange flash of familiarity that she felt once again, she didn't recognize him. The naked man was a total stranger.

Maggie definitely would have remembered meeting a man like this one before—even *with* his clothes on.

He was tall and almost sinfully well built, all hard muscles and not an extra ounce of fat on him anywhere. And in his current state of undress, she had an extremely accurate view of all of his anywheres. He had extremely broad shoulders and powerful-looking arms. He had one of those sexy washboard stomachs leading down into narrow hips, a perfect butt, and lean, long legs.

He had thick dark brown hair that he now ran his fingers through, taming it somewhat as he pushed it back from his face. He had dark hair on his chest and other places as well.

Maggie hurriedly brought her gaze back up to his face. His nose was gracefully shaped with almost elegant nostrils. His cheekbones were prominent, too, as was the firm set of his jaw and chin. He had a scar on his cheek-bone, underneath his left eye, making him look faintly dangerous. But it was his dark brown eyes that held her attention. They seemed to burn her with their intensity and fire.

Without question, he was the most gorgeous naked madman she'd ever come face-to-face with. Not that she'd come face-to-face with many madmen, clothed or otherwise, in her life.

"It's me," he told her, holding out his arms as if that would make her recognize him. "Chuck."

"I'm sorry," she said. "But . . . I don't know you."

He stared at her, confusion in his eyes. "You don't?"

"Maybe you have the wrong house," she suggested hopefully.

The man shook his head. "No. Maybe I have the wrong—" He interrupted himself. "What's the date?"

"Thursday, November twentith."

"No, the year. What's the *year?*"

She told him.

He swore sharply, clearly upset, and Maggie reached behind her for the telephone, ready to dial 911 at the least little eruption of violence.

"The damned prototype overshot my mark by three years," he muttered, talking more to himself than to her as he paced back and forth on her patio. His words didn't make sense, but he was insane. His words weren't *supposed* to make sense. "Okay. Okay. So here I am. Better early than late."

As Maggie watched he took a deep breath and seemed to pull himself together then looked up at her again.

"I'm Chuck Della Croce," he introduced himself. "And you don't know me, and . . . I'm naked." There was a flash of chagrin in his eyes, as well as something that might have been amusement. "God, talk about making a good first impression."

"Is there someone you want me to call to come and get you?" Maggie asked, trying to remember what she knew about insanity. Was she supposed to back slowly away, speak softly, and keep from looking directly into his eyes? Or was that what she was supposed to do if she encountered a wild animal? Something about this man was wild, that much was for sure.

The man shook his head, again trying to tame his hair, combing it back with his fingers. "No, I'm right where I want to be." He snorted. "Give or take three years." He took another deep breath. "I could sure use a pair of pants, though." He seemed to notice the gash on his shoulder for the first time, along with the dirt that covered him, and he swore again, softly this time. "And maybe the use of your garden hose to wash up?"

Maggie hesitated.

"Please?" he added, gazing up at her.

What *was* it about him . . . ?

"I don't think I have any pants that will fit you," she told him. "But I'll look. And yes. Use the hose. It's in the—"

"I know where the hose is, Mags." Sure enough, he seemed to know that the hose and the spigot it was attached to was inside the little garden shed built onto the side of her house.

Maggie felt a chill run up her spine. How did he know that the hose was there instead of outside, the way it was for most houses? And how did he know her name?

Mail. He could have checked her mail. Or looked in the phone book. There were a zillion ways he could have learned her name. And she'd used the hose to water her fig tree just the night before, after the searing southwestern sun had set. He could have been watching. He might well have been watching for days.

The thought was a creepy one, and she shivered again as she shut and locked the window. Why was she doing this? She should just call the police and have this man removed from her yard. There was surely some Phoenix city ordinance that prohibited people from walking around naked in other people's yards.

She carried the phone with her as she went into the guest bedroom and opened the closet door. The small space was jammed with boxes of Christmas ornaments and Halloween decorations and a rack of clothing that she couldn't bring herself to throw out. But there was nothing inside that would fit a tall, solidly built man.

Maggie had a muscle or two herself from taking long bike rides around the city, but at five feet two, she was seriously height-challenged. She bought her clothes from the petite rack at the store. No, nothing she owned would even begin to cover the handsome, naked, extremely tall madman in her backyard.

Her bathrobe. That might at least cover him. Of course, it was pink with little flowers on the lapels. A friend had bought it for her, as a kind of a joke. Maggie was not and never had been the pink-with-little-flowers type. She would be embarrassed even to show it to him.

Still, it was the only thing she had that would fit him.

And hey. He was crazy. Maybe he'd like it.

Unless . . .

Maggie quickly pulled one of the boxes down from the shelf. It was the wrong box, but there were only two others marked CHRISTMAS, so she knew she didn't have far to search.

She found what she was looking for in the second box she took from the closet.

A Santa Claus suit. Huge red pants with a drawstring waist and a red jacket with fluffy white trim and a black plastic belt sewn directly onto it.

It was big enough, that was for sure.

She carried it back to the bathroom window. Out in the yard, Chuck What's-his-name had somehow hooked the hose to the old clothesline. He'd also managed to make the water come out in a spray. He stood underneath it, as if it were a shower, water streaming onto his head and down his face. The water made his muscles glisten and shine.

Maggie felt like some kind of voyeur, watching him like that. She was grateful her yard was enclosed by solid wooden fencing and that none of her immediate neighbors in this little Phoenix development had more than a single-story house. No one could see the naked man taking a shower in her backyard.

Except for her.

He opened his eyes and looked directly up at her—catching her staring at him.

Quickly, she turned away from the window, rummaging through her linen closet for one of her older towels. She found one that was worn and tossed it down, directly onto the center of the sun-blistered picnic table on her patio. She tossed the Santa suit down too.

"Thanks." He grabbed the towel as he moved to shut off the water.

Maggie tried not to watch him as he dried himself,

but it proved impossible. She had to move away from the window and gaze up at the bathroom ceiling to keep herself from staring.

What *was* it about this guy? she found herself wondering again. The man was matter-of-factly casual about his nakedness, but so would she be, if she were as physically fit as he was.

"Hey, Maggie?"

She peeked out the window, relieved to see that he had pulled on the bright red pants and tied the drawstring around his waist. They were baggy and much too short, but at least they covered him.

He was holding the Santa jacket up, looking at it with barely concealed horror.

"Don't you have a T-shirt I can borrow?" he asked her. "I'm going to roast if I have to put this on."

Actually, she had a number of oversized T-shirts that she wore to bed as nightshirts. "Hang on," she told him, and carefully closing and locking the window, she went into her bedroom. She grabbed one of her T-shirts from her drawer. On second thought, she took a comb from the top of her dresser as well.

He was sitting on the edge of the picnic table, drumming the fingers of both hands on the rough wood, waiting for her when she returned to the bathroom window. She tossed down the T-shirt and comb, and again, he thanked her politely.

He was clean now, and while the lack of dirt and blood made him look slightly less certifiable, the Santa pants took him well in the opposite direction.

But as he ran the comb through his dark hair, he looked up at her again and his eyes were clear and sharp.

"Will you take a walk over to the park with me?" he asked. "I'd like to talk to you about—"

"I'm sorry," she cut him off. "I have to get back to work."

He saw right through her excuse. "We could go somewhere less deserted," he suggested. "That restaurant around the corner—you know, the place you like to go for Mexican food."

"Tia's?"

"Is that what it's called? The place that makes that killer black-bean soup?"

How did *he* know black-bean soup was her favorite? This was getting downright weird. "That's Tia's. But you'll never get in without shoes on."

"I'll improvise."

Still, Maggie shook her head. "I'm sorry, I really can't—"

"Look, you don't have to walk over there with me. I'll go first. You can meet me there in twenty minutes. In the bar. In public. I won't get near you. No tricks, I swear."

"Why do you need to talk to me so badly? And how do you know my name?"

Chuck Della Croce gazed up at her silently for a moment. Then he dropped his bomb.

"I'm from the future," he told her almost flatly, matter-of-factly. "And in the future, we're friends. I'm a time traveler, Mags, and I need your help to save the world."

❖———————❖

Chuck watched as Maggie took a fortifying sip of her beer.

"Okay," she said. "All right." She pressed her palms flat against the table in the bar in Tia's restaurant, as if needing to feel the solidness of the wood beneath her hands. "Let me see if I've got this straight. I'm supposed to believe that you're some kind of a rocket-scientist genius type who's invented a time machine. Despite the fact that you look like some crazy, homeless guy wearing Santa pants, a Phoenix Film Marathon T-shirt, and ugly cardboard shoes."

Chuck glanced down at the cardboard and string sandals he'd made. He didn't think they were *that* bad—considering the choice of materials he'd had to work with.

"I'm supposed to believe that you've zipped back here in your little Runaround time-travel pod—"

"Runabout," he corrected her.

"—from seven years in the future, where you and I just happen to be friends."

She didn't believe him. Why should she believe him? Time travel. It seemed so science fiction. She was gazing at him with such cynical disbelief in her eyes, he couldn't help but smile.

He smiled as he hid his trembling hands, as he fought to keep these waves of emotion from overpowering him.

God, three hours ago, he hadn't thought he'd ever smile again. Three hours ago, the woman sitting across the table from him had bled to death in his arms. Three hours ago, she'd used her own body as a shield, taking bullets meant to kill *him*. Three hours ago, he'd escaped through the ventilation system in the Data Tech building, running for his life.

The pungent odor of gunpowder and blood still lingered in his nostrils despite the shower he'd taken underneath Maggie's garden hose. Boyd was dead. Maggie had seen Chuck's best friend and security chief take a bullet in the back of the head. She'd told him about it before she, too, had died. He was still shaking from all that he'd been through, all that he'd seen. Destruction of his lab. Death on a massive, global scale in the form of a bomb taking out the White House, and with it, the President of the United States. And death on a smaller, far more personal level too.

Chuck gazed at Maggie, shifting slightly in his seat, trying to rid himself of the disturbing memories of death on an extremely personal level. He took a deep breath.

None of that had happened yet. And he was here to make damn sure it wouldn't happen again. This time around was going to be different. He'd never tried to tamper with time before, not to this degree. He had no idea how easy or hard it was going to be. But easy or hard, it didn't matter. He was determined to set things right and keep innocent people from dying.

But for right now, all he wanted to do was gaze into Maggie's light brown eyes. He didn't care that they were filled with skepticism. He didn't care that one graceful eyebrow was lifted in disbelief. He'd expected as much from her. She was so straightforward, so honest and down-to-earth, he would have been surprised had she believed him without an argument.

Chuck was ready to argue with her all night, if she

wanted. He didn't care. He just wanted to look at her. She was just so beautifully alive.

His hand was shaking as he picked up his mug of coffee, so he set it back on the table without taking a sip. He wanted to touch her hand, or the soft smoothness of her cheek, but he didn't dare.

She thought he was nuts.

"So if what you're saying is true, there's some kind of time machine—this Runabout thing—sitting in my backyard?"

Chuck shifted in his seat. "Actually, no—"

"No."

The look in her eyes made him want to laugh, but he was afraid if he started, he wouldn't be able to stop.

"Of course not," she continued. "Come on, tell me why it's not still there, and make it a really good one."

"I had to program the return jump in my lab, before I left, and since I knew this was going to be a one-way trip, I set it up to self-destruct," Chuck told her. "See, there's a long recharging delay between jumps. If the mechanism is engaged too soon, the device malfunctions, and the Runabout is destroyed."

"Of course," she said. "I should have known."

"It's the truth."

"It sounds like anything but. I mean, *really*, Chuck. You've traveled back in time because some evil government agents from some ridiculous-sounding organization—"

"Wizard-9," he supplied.

"Yeah. Right. These guys from Wizard-whatever got their nefarious hands on your time machine and managed to plant some kind of bomb in the White House that killed the president and his entire staff, including the Speaker of the House, in order to trigger a political coup." When she said it that way, it sounded like the bad plot of a comic book.

"The coup is just my theory. I didn't stick around long enough to find out if I was right."

"So you've come back in time to stop yourself from developing time travel, in order to prevent this assassination. Have I left anything out?"

"That's about it in a nutshell," he told her.

"Why not just go back in time and warn the people at the White House about the bomb? Why stop the entire project before it even starts?"

He answered her gravely, as if her question were serious. "I figured if I did only that, the door through time would still be left open. This way, the problem of unauthorized time tampering is solved once and for all."

Chuck had actually considered going back to his childhood, back before the time when the idea of time travel first flashed into his head. But he couldn't be sure that a change made that far in his past would be enough to alter his entire future. He knew he had only one shot, and he had to be damn well certain it would work.

Maggie sat back in her chair. "Meanwhile, while all this was happening in Metropolis, Superman couldn't do anything to stop the evil Wizard-9 agents, because he had been struck down by a bullet made of kryptonite."

Chuck had to laugh. "I'd almost forgotten how sarcastically funny you used to be."

"What, I'm not as funny seven years from now?"

He couldn't quite meet her gaze, unwilling to tell her the truth. He realized he was nervously drumming his fingers on the table and he forced himself to stop, to sit calmly, without moving.

She leaned forward. "Come on, Futureman. What am I like seven years from now? Does my freelance-writing business finally earn enough to pay my mortgage? Do I move into one of those big houses on Camelback Mountain? Do I have any kids? A rich, handsome husband? No, wait a sec. Don't tell me. *You*'re my husband, right?"

"Wrong." He looked across the table at her. She was incredibly pretty, but she didn't know it. She'd probably never know it.

Her hair was brown and at from a distance it seemed to be nothing special. It was only up close that one could see that it hung in shining waves around her face, long and thick and glistening. Her eyes, too, were an average shade of brown, but they sparkled and danced when she smiled and laughed. Her face was long, with a delicate cleft in her chin, her jaw strong and almost square. Her nose turned up very slightly at the end.

She was gorgeous in a girl-next-door kind of way, with a brilliant smile that could light up the darkest night.

She was funny and smart and sweet. And incredibly sexy.

He'd been wildly attracted to her from the very moment he'd first set eyes on her—seven years ago, his time. And she'd been attracted to him. It had happened this time around, too, despite the fact that she doubted his sanity. He could feel the familiar sexual pull, even now, each time she looked into his eyes.

If history was going to repeat itself, she would learn

to hide that attraction from him, letting him see only friendly warmth in her eyes. But he was here to make sure that history *didn't* repeat itself.

"Two years from now you'll marry a man named Albert Ford," he finally told her. "An accountant. It won't work out. One of the last times we spoke, you told me you were waiting for the divorce papers to arrive. I think the whole thing was pretty nasty. So, yeah, it's been a while since you've made very many jokes."

Maggie stood up. "Well, this was more fun than I've had since the last time I played with my Magic Eight Ball."

He stood up, too, and Maggie felt a flare of panic. Shoot, she'd forgotten how big this guy was. When she'd come into the bar, he was already sitting down. But now he towered over her.

He sat down quickly, as if he could read the sudden fear in her eyes. "I'm sorry," he murmured. "I didn't mean to—"

"I have to go," she told him. It was the truth. She'd already lost more than an hour of her workday thanks to him, and she had a deadline to make, writing copy for an upscale landscaper's brochure. She should be thinking of ways to describe mulching and privacy shrubbery instead of wasting her time with incredible tales of presidential assassination and Wizard-9 agents told by a too-handsome escapee from a mental hospital.

She was a fool for coming in the first place. It was her attraction to this man that made her meet him here—and that made her an even bigger fool. What did she honestly think? That he was potential boyfriend material? A lunatic who walked around naked and thought he came from the future?

She'd never considered herself a particularly good judge of character when it came to men, but this situation was a no-brainer.

He was trying to hide his desperation the same way he'd tried to hide the fact that his hands were shaking. He was good at hiding things. When he spoke, his voice was calm, and when he looked up at her again, his manner was cool, almost distant. He'd even managed to lose some of the heat in his liquid brown eyes. "Maggie, what can I say to make you believe me? To make you stay?"

He was remarkably attractive with the restaurant's dim mood lighting casting shadows across his rugged features. He was good-looking despite the grim set to his mouth and the clenched tightness of his jaw.

It was funny, she'd never found the Clint Eastwood type of man so attractive before. She usually preferred a Tom Hanks. Sensitivity with a healthy dose of good humor usually won out over ominous, smoldering danger any day.

And this man sitting across from her *did* exude danger with the start of a five o'clock shadow darkening the lower half of his face, his damp longish hair swept back from his forehead, and blood from his wounded shoulder seeping through the thin cotton of his borrowed T-shirt. Fortunately, from where she was sitting, she couldn't see the Santa pants.

She pulled the strap of her handbag over her shoulder. "Well, you might've tried telling me that I'm going to win the lottery next year rather than all that doom and gloom about a failed marriage."

He shook his head. "But that wouldn't be true."

Maggie felt a flash of pity. Poor crazy guy. He actually believed all that he'd told her.

"I really have to go." She looked down at her half-empty glass of beer and his barely touched coffee. "I don't suppose you have the money to pay for this."

He looked embarrassed. "Not at this time, no. I used an early prototype to make the leap back. It was in my basement—the Wizard-9 agents didn't know about it. It was less sophisticated than the final version of the Runabout, and because of that I could take nothing with me—not even my clothes."

"Well, *there*'s a convenient explanation for why you were walking around naked." Maggie opened her purse, took a twenty-dollar bill from her wallet, and set it down on the table. "Keep the change, Nostradamus, all right?"

"I'll pay you back."

"Don't bother."

"I will. I'll bring it to you tomorrow."

His quiet words stopped her, and she turned to look back at him. "I'd rather you just stayed away from my house. In fact, if I see you again, I'm going to have to call the police and—"

"Then maybe I better warn you. We're going to meet for the first time in just a few days," he told her. "At Data Tech's Thanksgiving party."

Maggie took a step back toward him, startled. Data Tech. She'd recently signed a contract with Data Tech to write a prospectus for a public offering. And the ink on a second contract with the software giant—this one for editing an annual report—was barely dry. And she *had* received an invitation to the annual Thanksgiving party at Data Tech. She'd already decided to go to the Tuesday-night affair, to schmooze with her new clients and to sniff around and see if there were any other potential projects requiring her talents.

"You won't meet me," Chuck told her. "At least not exactly. You'll meet my younger self—Charles. Dr. Charles Della Croce."

"Your *younger* self . . ." Maggie had to laugh. "Of course. If you're from the future, then it stands to reason that there's another you—a younger you—running around somewhere."

He didn't crack a smile. "Look, I know this sounds crazy to you."

"Well, there you go," Maggie said. "We've finally agreed on something."

"I really need your help."

"Chuck, you need help—that's for *sure*, but I'm not the one who can give it to you." Silently she cursed herself for not just turning and walking away. Instead she sat down across from him again, knowing she was going to kick herself over and over as she was forced to work late into the night to make up for this lost time. "Let me make some phone calls, call a few friends, find you a doctor who can—"

His fingers started drumming impatiently on the table again. "Nostradamus," he said suddenly.

"Excuse me?"

Chuck realized he was doing it again. He was tapping his fingers, and he stilled them, consciously trying hard to rein in his impatience. "You called me Nostradamus," he told Maggie, gripping the edge of the table instead.

"And you're right—I know your future. All I have to do is remember something . . . I don't know, some newsworthy event that happened after November twentith this year."

Maggie closed her eyes as she pressed one hand against her forehead, as if she had a headache. She sighed and opened her eyes again. "I'm going to have to go," she said again. "I can't worry about where you're going to spend the night or what you're going to eat or—"

"There was a plane crash," Chuck suddenly remembered. "I think it was November. Yes—it was about a week before Thanksgiving. It hasn't happened yet, has it?"

Maggie threw her hands into the air. "Jeez, I don't know. Maybe. Where was it? A private plane went down a few days ago in the Rockies."

"No," Chuck said. "This was major. This was a commercial flight out of New York, heading to London. A terrorist's bomb went off when the plane came in for a landing. It was awful—hundreds of people died."

Maggie pushed back her chair and stood up, opening her purse one more time. "God knows I can't afford this, but . . ." She put another two twenties on the table. "Stay someplace warm tonight, Chuck. And think about getting some help."

He picked up the money and held it out to her. "Maggie, I don't need this. Honestly. I've got access to a bank account."

But Maggie was backing away. "Good-bye, Chuck."

"I'll be here at Tia's, every afternoon at this time." He didn't raise his voice to call after her, but it carried to her just the same. "If you change your mind, you can find me here in the bar."

Maggie pushed open the door and stepped out into the late-afternoon heat, resisting the urge to turn one last time and look back.

TWO

It was after five o'clock on Friday when Maggie finished her meeting with the Data Tech vice-presidents. There were four of them, and each had had his own idea about how the company's current prospectus should be written.

Working for more than one boss was a potential nightmare, but she'd learned a long time ago simply to smile, nod, take notes—and then write the darn thing the way *she* envisioned it. She'd give each of them an individual call to tell them how she'd incorporated their personal suggestions into her final draft. With any luck, everyone would be happy.

More than one of the VPs had hinted that if this project went well, she'd be offered a salaried position with the company. After three years of self-employment, the thought of a steady paycheck, employer-paid benefits, and scheduled vacations was tempting.

The Data Tech headquarters was an easy commute from her house. The company was a fairly affluent one, and it showed in the design of the building. Tasteful Southwestern decor graced the spacious three-story lobby, allowing office workers, clients, and guests three different views of the magnificent metal sculpture of a flock of birds taking flight that seemed to lift off from the lobby floor.

As Maggie joined the small crowd of people waiting for the elevator going down, she turned to look back at the sculpture. The people she'd met here were friendly and happy. She'd been told about a workout room in the basement, and that the food in the cafeteria was near gourmet quality. And salary raises were regular and generous. No, she wouldn't mind working here at all.

The elevator door slid open, and she turned to see that it was already crowded. Only a few people got on—there was no room for her.

The crowd shifted slightly, and then she saw him.

Chuck Della Croce. The gorgeous madman.

He was standing in the elevator, fully dressed in a respectable-looking business suit. His hair was shorter, his mouth less tight and grim, but it was him, wasn't it? He was facing her, and as she stared at him he briefly met her gaze.

There was nothing there. No flicker of awareness, no sign of recognition. Nothing.

Because it wasn't Chuck Della Croce. It was his "younger self," Charles. And this younger man hadn't met her yet.

The door closed, and he disappeared from view.

Of all the ridiculous, silly thoughts! Of *course* it wasn't Chuck Della Croce or even *Charles* Della Croce. It was simply someone who looked a lot like him.

She was losing it, big time. As if time travel really existed. As if she actually believed Chuck's delusional ravings.

Still, Maggie moved quickly to the railing and looked down into the lobby. As she watched, the tall dark-haired man who may or may not have been Charles Della Croce came out of the elevator and walked across the tile floor, past the flying birds, talking to another man.

Both men were pulling off their ties, and Chuck . . . Charles—whoever he was—shrugged out of his jacket in preparation for heading out into the late-afternoon sunshine.

From this angle, this height, the top of his head sure looked familiar. Too bad he wasn't naked—that would have clinched it. If he hadn't been wearing his clothes, she would have known without a doubt whether or not this was the same man who'd pounded on her door the afternoon before.

And then he laughed at something the other man said. Maggie caught only the briefest profile of his face, but it was enough to make her heart nearly stop beating. Whoever he was, when he smiled like that, he was impossibly handsome.

As she watched, the man pushed open the heavy glass doors and headed toward the parking lot.

By the time Maggie reached the lobby herself, he was long gone, and she'd nearly succeeded in convincing herself that seeing this man was a mere coincidence. So this guy looked like her gorgeous madman. A lot of men did. The phrase *tall, dark, and handsome* hadn't become a cliché without reason.

Still, she couldn't keep herself from stopping at the main reception area. "Excuse me, is there a Charles Della Croce working here?"

The woman behind the reception desk keyed the name into her computer. "Yes," she said. "Dr. Della Croce. He's upstairs in research and development. Oops, I'm sorry—I see he's just left the building. Would you like to leave a message for him?"

But Maggie was already backing away. "No. No, thank you."

Okay. There had to be a reasonable explanation for this. Such as, the madman knew he looked like this scientist and had borrowed his persona. She knew nearly all there was to know about Data Tech, after all. Most of the work done in their R&D labs dealt with computer software, not time travel. In fact, there was no mention of time travel in any of the information Maggie had been given about the corporation.

She headed quickly out to the parking lot and unlocked her little car.

It had been sitting in the sun for hours, and the temperature inside was ovenlike. Maggie pulled down all the windows and turned the AC on full power as she headed onto the main road.

What if he were telling the truth?

The thought was a tiny one, but it niggled at the back of her mind obstinately.

He wasn't telling the truth, she told herself firmly. He was insane. And she would be, too, if she started believing him.

The air coming out of the vents was starting to feel cooler, so she closed the windows. She turned on the radio, too, determined not to think about anything at all until she got home. Then she'd think only about dinner. And after dinner, she'd finish up the copy for that landscaping brochure and—

". . . reports now say that the airliner carrying over three hundred passengers went down around two A.M., London time, over the Atlantic." The normally ebullient country-station DJ sounded sober and solemn. "I repeat, World Airlines flight 450 from New York to London exploded in midair over the Atlantic Ocean around two o'clock this morning. There are believed to be no survivors."

She was only a block away from her house, but Maggie had to pull over to the side of the road. She could barely breathe despite the fact that the air conditioner had fully kicked in.

How could Chuck have known? Somehow he'd *known.* . . .

"The investigating agencies have issued a short statement saying that the explosion was the result of a terrorist act. Apparently attempts were made to negotiate with the terrorists onboard. A tape of those conversations will be released at a later date."

Terrorists. A terrorist's bomb brought the plane down. Chuck had told her about it. He'd warned her. But she'd done nothing. She'd called no one.

And over three hundred people had died.

Maggie did a U-turn, tires squealing, heading for Tai's.

❖━━━━━━❖

Chuck saw Maggie pull up outside of the restaurant. She was driving much too fast, and he knew she was here because she'd heard the news reports about Flight 450.

He went out on the sidewalk to meet her.

As he moved into the late-afternoon sunshine he was struck again, as he had been repeatedly since yesterday, by the sense of freedom he felt. For the first time in years he was able to go wherever he pleased without a pair of bodyguards watching his back.

"I tried to warn them," he told Maggie before she could say even a word. "I remembered it was World Airlines, and I called them right after you left last night, but the jet had already departed from Kennedy Airport. I was too late."

"How did you know?" she asked. There was suspicion in her eyes, and her face was almost ashen.

"I told you how I knew," he said quietly, aware that the clerk from the nearby convenience store had come out onto the sidewalk to have a cigarette and was eyeing them curiously. "Why don't you come inside, and I'll buy you a drink. You look as if you could use something."

She backed away from him. "You knew because you're one of them. You're one of the terrorists who planted that bomb."

"Oh, come on. You don't believe that. That's ridiculous."

"And your claim that you're a time traveler isn't . . . ?"

She did a double take then, as if really looking at him for the first time. The Santa Claus pants and makeshift sandals were gone. Her eyes were wide as she took in his jeans, his nearly brand-new polo shirt, and the expensive leather of the new cowboy boots he'd picked up just this morning. He knew he looked a lot different from the wild-eyed man who'd pounded on her door just over twenty-four hours ago.

"Where did you get those clothes?"

"I'm not a terrorist," he told her. "In fact, my phone call to World Airlines saved lives. The way it really happened—the way I remember it happening the first time around—the bomb didn't go off until the plane was coming in for a landing. It took out an entire terminal at Heathrow. Five hundred people on the ground died, as well as the three hundred and forty-two passengers on the plane."

"Where did you get those clothes?"

He could tell from the look in her eyes that she wasn't buying any of this. Okay. They'd start small. They'd start with his clothes.

"That was easy. I went home. To *Charles*'s home. I know where I used to hide the key, and his clothes are all my size—because I'm him. This shirt is a color I never liked—I won't miss it. The jeans I've already missed. I remember that I wondered what happened to them. See, there's this strange memory thing that happens when you change the past. You get something called residual memories and—"

"Just stop!" she said fiercely. "Stop with the time-travel crap. I want to know who you really are. I want to know the *truth*."

"Maggie, I swear, I've told you nothing but the truth."

Maggie spun away from him, heading toward the pay

phone that was under the overhang of the convenience-store roof. "That's it. I'm calling the police."

He caught her arm. "Don't. Please. I didn't have anything to do with that plane crash. I was just trying to show you that I *am* from the future by telling you what was going to happen."

Maggie was scared. She didn't know what to think, what to do. She wanted this out of her hands. This man looked so normal, dressed in jeans and a casual faded-green polo shirt. His hair was neatly combed and his chin was smooth from a recent shave. He didn't look like any kind of a madman today. He looked like the kind of man who would stand out in a crowd—the kind of man she'd make an effort to meet face-to-face.

Well, she was face-to-face with him right now, all right.

"Let go of me or I'll scream," she whispered.

"Two more days," Chuck said. His gaze was steady but no less intense as he looked into her eyes. "Please, Mags. Give me just two more days to change your mind."

She shook her head. "Two days isn't going to make a difference in the way I feel."

"Yes, it will. I remembered something else that happened. The news came just two days after the reports of the downed jet."

She closed her eyes. "Oh, please, don't tell me anyone else is going to die—"

"Not if I can help it," he told her. "I already called the seismology center in California, telling them to release a warning. There's going to be an earthquake—a pretty bad one. The epicenter's in Whittier. The reports

should be coming in right about this time on Sunday."
He smiled then, a slight twisting of his lips. "Even *you*'ve
got to admit that there's no way I could be responsible
for an earthquake."

Maggie stood in her living room, staring at the tele-
vision.

An earthquake. The TV news anchors were report-
ing an earthquake, just the way the madman had said.
Exactly the way he had said.

The epicenter *was* in Whittier. The quake registered
a 6.2 on the Richter scale.

Amazingly, the news anchors reported, as far as they
knew at this point, no one had been killed or even badly
injured. Apparently, an unidentified caller had predicted
the quake. Since this was California, they said with a
smile, and conditions for an earthquake had been right,
the caller had been taken seriously enough for them to
use the emergency broadcast system to warn the city's
residents.

Oddly enough, the call was traced to a pay phone in
downtown Phoenix, Arizona, of all places.

Maggie slowly sat down, right in the middle of her
living-room floor.

She'd spent the entire weekend trying to work, but
barely able to. She'd kept coming back to the TV and
the news reports of the plane crash. To the pictures of
the people who had lost their lives when the terrorists'
bomb had gone off.

But now the screen was filled with live video footage
taken during the earthquake.

The madman had accurately predicted the future not once but twice.

The madman very likely wasn't mad at all.

The telephone rang. Maggie wasn't a time traveler from the future herself, but she knew exactly who was on the other end.

She crawled across the carpeting to her coffee table and pressed the mute button on the remote control as she picked up her cordless phone.

"Where are you?" she asked. "We need to talk."

"I'm at Tia's," Chuck's soft baritone voice told her. "I was hoping you'd let me come by."

Maggie looked at the soundless pictures of the earthquake's destruction on the TV. A road had been nearly ripped in half, the blacktop crumpled and folded.

"I'd rather meet you at the restaurant," she told him.

He didn't hesitate. "Fair enough. I'll get a table for dinner."

"Order me a tequila," Maggie said. "I think I'm going to need one."

"I called it the Wells Project," Chuck said.

"As in H. G. Wells?"

He nodded. "Yeah. I'd been working on the theory for years—literally since I was a kid. But it wasn't until a little more than three years from now that I came up with the breakthrough equation.

"I got approval from Data Tech to run with it, but when the time came to actually build the Runabout, we had to look outside the company for funding." He frowned down at the last of the refried beans that remained on his plate. His cheese enchilada was long gone. "That's when I was approached by Wizard-9."

"They're *really* called Wizard-9?"

Chuck had to smile at Maggie's expression of disbelief. "Yeah, they're really called Wizard-9. It's a pretty powerful organization. Covert too. And dangerous as hell. Not even the president himself knew about this group. Or if he knew about them, he didn't know what they had planned, that was for sure."

He took a deep breath. "Anyway, they provided Data Tech—and me—with the money necessary to build the Runabout in return for the right to regulate use of the device. They told me that time travel could be a deadly weapon, and without regulation, there was always the possibility that terrorists or criminals could get their hands on the Runabout and change the course of history. I suspected they were interested in more than regulating the project, but I let myself be blind to that. All I cared about was making the Wells Project a reality."

He stopped himself from drumming his fingers on the table before he even started. All this was his fault. He'd let Wizard-9 get involved. He was responsible for everything that happened as a result of that. He was responsible for all those deaths, for Maggie's death. . . .

"Turns out that the agents from Wizard-9 *were* the terrorists," he told her grimly. "They used the Runabout without my authorization to go back in time and set a bomb at the White House. The president, the vice president . . . everyone was killed."

"How did you know?" Maggie frowned. "I mean, if the agents from Wizard-9 didn't tell you they were going back in time, how could you even know that everything didn't happen the way it was supposed to happen? How did you know they were responsible?"

"I probably *wouldn't* have known, if I hadn't been doing experimentation in something that I called 'double memories.'" Chuck pushed his plate forward as he explained. "I just ate a cheese enchilada, right?"

She glanced down at his plate and nodded.

"You have a memory of me eating that cheese enchilada. If you were paying close attention, you probably have a memory of me burning my tongue. You have a memory of sitting across from me, eating your blackbean soup and a salad. You remember the waitress—the scent of her perfume, perhaps. You have memories of all those things, right?"

She nodded again, her gaze never leaving him as she tried to follow where he was leading. He liked having her full attention. It had been a long time. The Maggie from his time had been distracted and unhappy for the past few years as she struggled to make her failing marriage work. But this was before all that. This was before she married that fool. This was before she discovered that the sizzling attraction that sparked every time she looked in Chuck's eyes wasn't what she wanted.

"Now, suppose I were to go into the men's room and sneak out the window to the alley where I supposedly keep my Runabout. And suppose I were to travel back in time just an hour or so," Chuck told her, "where I would intercept you on your way into Tia's and take you somewhere else—like up to the Pointe—for dinner. Suppose I order a couple of steaks and baked potatoes and we eat that. I changed history, right? Steaks and potatoes replaced enchiladas and black-bean soup. *But*. Here's the strange part.

"I've found that when time has been tampered with—and my going back in time and changing these things, as inconsequential as they seem, *is* time tampering—people are left with residual memories. These residual memories—or memories of how it actually happened the first time around—provide time travelers and those people affected by the time travel with *double memories*.

"Your most vivid memory would be of your steak and potato, but you would *also* remember the black-bean soup. It'd be foggy almost as if it were a dream, but it'd be back there. Double memories. Of course, since I'm the person who did the actual time traveling, both of my memories will be clear and vivid, because both events actually *happened* to me."

She nodded. "That makes sense."

"If you concentrate, you may be able to find a residual memory of what you did immediately after you heard about the earthquake the first time around."

Maggie closed her eyes for a moment, frowning slightly. When she opened her eyes, they were wide with surprise. "I stayed home and watched the news all night," she said. "Oh, that's so *weird*."

"That's right." Chuck gestured around them at the restaurant. "This isn't the way it originally happened, so you have double memories both of being home alone, and of spending the night with me."

Her eyes flashed as she met his gaze, but she looked away immediately, and he realized the implications of what he'd said. He'd meant evening, not night. Spending the evening with him. Still, she didn't seem overly averse to his inadvertent suggestion that they spend the night together, and he felt a familiar hot flare of desire at the thought. God, he'd wanted her for so long.

He had to clear his throat before he spoke again. "A double memory can be so distant and dreamlike, I might not have noticed it if I hadn't been researching the phenomenon. But I knew something was wrong the morning that I woke up and turned on the TV and heard the first of the news reports about the White House bombing. I had a residual memory of that same morning that was very different. I could remember that I got up, turned on the TV while my coffee machine did its thing, and I felt disgusted by the lack of hard news. The biggest story even on CNN was the birth of some pop singer's baby. I still had that memory, and that's how I knew that time tampering was responsible for the assassination. And I knew it was the work of Wizard-9. They were the only ones besides me who had access to the Wells Project."

She was still watching him intently, her chin tucked into the palm of one hand. "So, okay," she said. "You've come back in time to change events that are going to occur in my future. But since you're *from* the future, all of the changes that you're going to make have already happened in your past. Shouldn't you already remember them?"

Chuck shook his head. "I understand what you're saying, but it doesn't work that way. I can't make one little change and know instantly how it's going to turn out unless I return to my own time. If I were to go back to my time after making a change, I'd have a sudden rush of very vivid double memories. I'd remember all the things that had happened differently in the seven years between now and then."

"So how will you know when you've made the changes you need to make?"

He gazed into her eyes. "I'll know."

"How? Because if you don't know the outcome, maybe you *have* done all you need—"

Chuck shook his head. "Simply coming back in time isn't enough. I need to create an event that will affect the life of my present-day self—of Charles. And as Charles does things differently, I'll have those new double memories—but only one by one as they happen in real time."

"Wait, you lost me. . . ."

Chuck shifted in his seat, leaning across the table, trying to make her understand. "Think of it on a physical level," he said. "Look at me. I'm here, I'm whole, right? If you were to X-ray me, you'd see I've never had a broken bone. I've lived to be forty-two years old and I'm still in one piece. But if I convinced you to go and push Charles—not me, but Charles—off the sidewalk and into oncoming traffic, my own X rays would suddenly be very different. You'd probably see multiple signs of healed fractures. And I'd probably have a couple more scars to show for it, even though it didn't happen to me. But think about it. It *did* happen to me, because he's *me.*"

He sat back in his seat, uncertain if she understood. "Memories, even double memories, work the same way. Until I actually change the past—until I convince you to actually push me into traffic, to continue with that rather grim example—I won't have a clue as to what's going to happen."

Her eyes didn't leave his face, her gaze sharp and probing. "Most people die when you push them into oncoming traffic. You're not here to ask me to help kill you, are you?"

Chuck considered trying to laugh her words off for about a tenth of a second, but the look in her eyes convinced him to be honest. This was Maggie he was talking to. She'd always been able to see right through him. "Actually, that's a solution I've considered," he told her seriously. "If Charles is gone, all those theories about time travel are gone too. It's a quick and easy fix. But remember what I just told you. What happens to him affects me. If he's dead, I'm dead too. I'm hoping to find another way."

Maggie took in a deep breath, letting it out in a burst of air. "Oh, man."

"I'm *going* to find another way," Chuck told her. "The agents from Wizard-9 tried to kill me. I don't want to give them the satisfaction of seeing me dead— even if the only way they'd remember me was in the faintest of double memories."

"That day you came," Maggie said. "There was blood on you. Your shoulder . . ."

His shoulder had only been scraped. Most of the blood had not been his own. Chuck took a sip of his soda. "I went to Data Tech that morning breathing fire, intending to use the Runabout to go back in time and prevent the bombing, but they were waiting for me."

He reached across the table for her hand, needing to touch her to eradicate the memories. He could still see her eyes, dimming as the life seeped from her body. He couldn't tell her all of it, but that didn't matter. He was going to make damned sure that it happened differently this time around.

"You were there," he whispered, "and somehow you knew they were gunning for me. You tried to warn me. You saved my life."

"Yeah, well, saving people's lives is one of those things I just happen to be good at—along with finding clothes for the naked time travelers who show up in my backyard." She was trying to make light of it, but he knew she was not unaffected by the touch of his hand.

He was not unaffected either. He laced their fingers together as he took a deep breath. "I need you to help me, Maggie."

She looked down at their hands, and then up, back into his eyes. "Okay." She nodded. "I'll help."

THREE

"Charles needs to be convinced to give up time-travel research," Chuck said. "I've been thinking about the best way to do this, and I keep coming back to you."

Maggie took a sip of her drink, feeling the warming kick of the tequila.

This seemed so unreal. She was sitting here, across this restaurant table from one of the most attractive men she'd ever met—discussing his plan for changing the future. He was going to tamper with time and change his own destiny in order to prevent Wizard-9 agents from overthrowing the U.S. government. She took another slug of her drink.

"Why me?"

"It's not going to be easy," he told her. "Developing time travel was always something of an obsession for me. What you'll need to do is to talk Charles into going back to school and getting his medical degree. You'll need to convince him—me—that there's plenty of work to be done in AIDS research. Charles needs to be talked into leaving Phoenix, into leaving Data Tech. And all his—my—research notes on time travel need to be destroyed."

Maggie shook her head. "I don't get it. Why do you need *me?* Why don't *you* just go to Charles and tell him everything that happened, convince him to give up his research that way?"

Chuck silently gazed at her. When he finally spoke, his voice was soft. "Because I remember how badly I wanted to develop time travel. And I'm not sure that loyalty to a president whose name he's never even heard is enough to make Charles give up his dream. Yeah, over a hundred people were killed in the bombing, but I know what he'll say. He'll say, think of the thousands who could be saved if time travel exists. He's never met anyone from Wizard-9. He won't understand the danger."

As Maggie looked into his eyes she knew he wasn't telling her everything. There was more, but he was leaving it out.

"But why me? Why should *I* be able to get through to him?"

He didn't answer right away. "Because there's something between us," he finally said quietly. "I feel it right now. I felt it the first time we met too. And Charles is going to feel it when he meets you at that Data Tech party on Tuesday."

Chemistry. He was talking about the sexual attraction that simmered between them. He was talking about using that attraction to knock his past self off his predestined path. If he really thought she could do *that,* he must be experiencing one hell of a powerful attraction.

Maggie was glad she was sitting down. She felt slightly weak in the knees. She hated to admit it, but she was feeling that attraction as well. Every time their eyes met. Every time their eyes *didn't* meet. It was always there, snapping and crackling around them like a live wire.

If you weren't careful, a live wire could kill you.

But what was he asking her to convince Charles of, really? Leave Phoenix, Chuck had said. Leave Data Tech. Did he expect her to leave Phoenix and Data Tech too? Did he expect her to do something like *marry* him? No, not him—Charles.

This was way too weird.

"Why do you call him Charles?" she asked. "I mean, he's really just you, only younger."

He shifted in his seat for about the thousandth time that evening. It was just one of the many ways his relentless energy slipped through the cracks of his self-control. Maggie knew well—even just from the few times she'd met him—that Chuck Della Croce was not a patient man. He didn't like to sit still, he didn't like to move slowly. Yet his intensity burned deeply, and he seemed to focus every ounce of his attention on every word she spoke and every move she made.

It was kind of scary actually—having him look at her that way.

What would it be like to make love to this man, to have that focus and attention in a purely sexual context? The thought made her mouth go dry, and she had to take another sip of her drink.

"Up until recently—this year in fact, your time," he

clarified, "nobody ever called me anything but Charles."
He smiled. It was really only a half smile, a slight twisting of one side of his mouth, yet it made him look even
more handsome. Thank God he didn't give her a full
grin. The force would've knocked her clear out of her
chair.

"But when I met you at that party," he continued,
"you decided right then and there that Charles was too
formal, and you started calling me Chuck."

Wait a minute. . . . "*I* did?"

"Yeah. Even though we didn't do more than date a
few times, you had a rather strong influence on my life."

She sat even farther forward. "We *dated*?"

"After we met at that Data Tech party, yeah, we went
out once or twice."

"Just . . . once or twice?"

He was cryptic. "At the time I didn't think we were
compatible, so I didn't pursue a relationship beyond
friendship."

She didn't get it. "But at that time you were Charles,
weren't you? I mean, you were more Charles than you
are now, seven years later. So if you didn't think we were
compatible then, why would Charles think we're compatible now? And what is it *exactly* that you want me to
do? All this talk about compatibility is making me a little
nervous."

"All I want you to do is meet him—me—*Charles*—at
that Data Tech party and let things happen as they're
supposed to. Only this time around, don't be so quick to
quit."

Maggie blinked. "Quit?"

He was drumming his fingers against the table and—as she'd seen him do before—he seemed suddenly to become aware of the sound, and forced himself to stop cold.

"Yeah," he said. "You were the one who broke it off between us."

Maggie had to laugh. This was too absurd. "Okay. Now we're getting into the really unbelievable stuff. The time travel I'm starting to be able to handle, but this . . . Nuh-uh. You're telling me that I broke up with you. That's insane. Why would I break up with you? You're brilliant, you're nice, you're polite—you seem socially adept—not too many eccentricities, give or take the finger-tapping thing. Your sense of humor needs a little work, but, you know, it's back there. It's hiding, but it seems solid enough. And, okay, maybe you need to work on being just a teeny bit warmer—maybe you need to practice stretching those lips into a smile in front of a mirror a few times a day. And speaking of mirrors, have you looked into one lately? You're gorgeous, Chuck. You're a twenty on a scale from one to ten. So what you're telling me is that you're perfect and *I* broke up with *you*. I don't think so, bub."

"It's true."

"And that's just you," she continued. "I haven't even started on *me*. I'm always the one in a relationship who hangs on until the bitter end, hoping for a happy ending. And oh, will you please look at me a little more closely? Maybe the light's not bright enough in here. You keep hinting at this instant animal attraction, love-at-first-sight doody, and—believe me, I know—I'm not the love-at-first-sight type. I mean, look at me. I'm just . . . not."

"Sorry, you're wrong," he said coolly. "Have *you* looked into a mirror lately? You're beautiful, Mags. This time around, I'm going to make damn sure you believe that."

Maggie rolled her eyes. "Oh, please."

He leaned forward, the intensity in his eyes sparking even hotter. "As far as I was concerned, the attraction factor alone was enough to keep us together for years, but you didn't agree."

"Are you sure you're talking to the right person?" she asked. "Because that doesn't sound like anything I'd ever say."

"I remember what you said." Chuck sat back and stirred the ice in his glass, his body language suddenly distant and closed. He glanced at her only briefly, keeping his eyes for the most part trained on his glass. "After we went out a few times, you told me . . . how did you say it? That you weren't interested in being physically intimate with a man who wouldn't be emotionally intimate with you—a man who wouldn't even talk about his day-to-day life, let alone his feelings."

"That sounds like me," Maggie conceded. Suddenly it all made sense. Chuck was attractive and intelligent and as sexy as hell, but he wasn't exactly the warm, fuzzy, sharing type. Even the level of intimacy needed for this conversation was difficult for him to handle—she could tell that from the way he was sitting, the way he wasn't meeting her gaze.

"There are some things I'm not sure I'm going to be

able to do any differently this time around," he said quietly. "And yet I'm asking you to do nearly everything differently." He forced a smile. "After seven years of friendship, I know you pretty well, Mags. I know you don't want me. If I could think of another way, short of kidnapping my own self . . ." He shook his head.

I know you pretty well, Mags.

Maggie was shaken. She was sitting and talking with a man who knew her far better than she knew him. How much better, she didn't know. She took a fortifying sip of her drink.

"So," she said, taking a deep breath. "Tell me honestly. Did I ever sleep with you—in my future and your past . . . ?" She rolled her eyes again. "Whoa, this is definitely Twilight Zone stuff."

He answered her seriously, quietly. "No. We never made love."

But he'd wanted to. He didn't say it in so many words, but she could see it in his eyes. He *still* wanted to.

"I have to go home now," Maggie told him. "I think my brain has just absorbed all the weirdness it can hold for one night."

She stood up, but then she stopped, looking back at him. "Do you have a place to stay tonight?"

He gave her another of those half smiles. "I don't suppose that's an invitation."

Her laughter sounded slightly hysterical. "Not a chance. But if you need some money for a motel room . . ."

"I'm fine. I know where Charles kept his extra bank-machine card. I'm all set for cash." He hesitated. "Can I walk you home?"

"Please don't."

Chuck nodded. "May I call you tomorrow?"

"Yeah. Call me." Maggie hurried away.

Maggie had three different work deadlines approaching at the rate of a speeding train, but she simply could not concentrate.

She couldn't stop thinking about Chuck.

His story was impossibly absurd. Time travel. A covert agency with plans to overthrow the government. It was insane.

Still, she found herself believing him.

And she found herself drifting out of focus as she sat in front of her computer, thinking not about his story, but about his eyes. About the way he looked at her, as if she were a tall glass of water and he was dying of thirst.

Getting involved with this man would be crazy. If everything he'd told her was true, he was from the future. He didn't belong in this time. There was already another one of him here. If he couldn't get back to his own time—and he'd implied that was true—he'd probably have to take on a new identity and . . . And if everything he'd told her *wasn't* true, if this all was some kind of giant con or scam, well, then she'd be twice the fool.

No, she was going to have to keep her emotions out of this. Friends. She was going to have to work to be sure they became nothing more than friends.

She closed her eyes tightly, trying to banish the picture of him standing naked in her yard.

The intensity in his liquid brown eyes was even harder to forget.

Unable to write an intelligible word, Maggie grabbed her purse and her car keys and headed over to Data Tech. She had to pick up a file she needed, and as long as she wasn't getting anything done, she might as well do it now.

This didn't have anything to do with wanting to get another look at the man Chuck had called Charles. She *wasn't* going to Data Tech to do something as asinine as to spy on Chuck's younger self.

As she made the turn into the Data Tech parking lot, she saw him. Charles Della Croce. Sitting behind the wheel of a gleaming white Honda, he was slipping on a pair of sunglasses as he braked to a stop before leaving the lot.

As he took a right, heading out toward downtown Scottsdale, Maggie made a quick U-turn, her tires squealing slightly on the hot asphalt as she followed him.

This was insane. This was not "picking up a file."

There were two other cars between her car and Charles. That was good. Not wanting him to notice that she was following him, she hung back slightly as he took another right turn.

He drove into the old-fashioned part of Scottsdale that was filled with quaint little shops and cafés and four-star restaurants.

Modern Phoenix and Scottsdale were made up of enormous shopping malls—places where, once inside, shoppers didn't have to face the fiery heat of the Southwestern sun as they went from store to store. But the older section of the city dated back to the days before air-conditioning, to the time of small-town America. The sidewalks here were no less busy because they were outside. They were crowded with tourists and the usual lunchtime business men and women.

Charles pulled into a parking space on a side street, and Maggie did the same, parking some distance away from him. He headed back toward the shops and restaurants on foot, and Maggie ran to keep up as he disappeared around the corner of a building.

The noontime sun was unseasonably warm for November, and even a brief sprint made her shirt stick uncomfortably to her body. As she rounded the corner she felt a rush of relief as she spotted Charles, his dark head a good four inches above the rest of the crowd. As she watched he crossed the street and went inside a trendy-looking little restaurant called Papa John's Eatery.

He sat down at a table near the front window. Maggie tried not to look too conspicuous as she pretended to look into the window of a Native American art and jewelry store while glancing back over her shoulder at the restaurant.

She saw a waiter approach Charles and hand him a cellular phone. He spoke for a moment, then handed the phone back, decidedly displeased. He said something to the waiter, gesturing at the place setting in front of him. The waiter nodded, and removed the extra silverware and glasses. It didn't take the detective ability of a Sherlock Holmes to figure out that Charles's lunch date had called to cancel.

As Maggie watched, Charles glanced at a menu and

ordered quickly and seemingly without much regard for what he would be eating.

She crossed the street, wanting to get nearer, needing to take a closer look. After all, she'd never seen Chuck and Charles in the same place at the same time. They could well be one and the same.

On a whim, she pulled open the door to Papa John's and went inside.

Charles was sitting at his table, paying no attention to what was going on around him, writing something in a small notebook.

Waving aside the waiter who was coming toward her, Maggie took a deep breath and headed for Charles, counting on the fact that she'd come up with some real-sounding excuse for being there when the time came to open her mouth.

"Hey, Chuck," she said, slipping into the chair next to his.

He looked up, startled.

Part of Maggie still hoped that this was one great big practical joke. He would meet her eyes sheepishly and grin and admit that Katy, Maggie's college roommate, had coerced him into playing this silly trick on her.

But there was absolutely no recognition in his eyes. None at all.

Dear God, he was Chuck—but he wasn't. His eyes were the same liquid shade of brown, his nose the same perfect shape. His hair was shorter, though, and the lines around his eyes and mouth were less pronounced. He looked younger. About seven years younger, she'd guess. *Exactly* seven years younger . . .

"I'm sorry," he said. His voice was the same too—a sexy baritone, resonant with a rich timbre. "I don't think we've . . . *Have* we met?"

His scar. The thin line that marked his left cheekbone, directly underneath his eye. It was gone. Or rather, perhaps more accurately, it hadn't yet appeared.

"Actually, no," Maggie said.

He was looking at her as if he were afraid she might be insane, and for a moment Maggie felt that could well be true. Sitting here like this, talking to him like this . . . This wasn't the way they'd met. Chuck had told her they'd first met at that party at Data Tech. She was probably messing things up royally, but now that she was here, now that she was face-to-face with Charles, she didn't want to leave.

She was fascinated. This *was* Chuck she was sitting across from. But he was a younger Chuck. A Chuck without that grim tightness to his mouth, without that tightly clenched jaw, and without that weary desperation in his eyes.

"I was being followed," she fabricated, praying that God would forgive her for lying, "by this really creepy guy—every time I turned around, he was right behind me. He was talking to himself, saying all kinds of really weird things. I saw you sitting in here all alone, and I thought maybe you wouldn't mind helping me out by pretending to be, you know, my significant other or something, so this guy will leave me alone once and for all . . . ?"

His gaze shifted and he squinted slightly as he looked out the window into the glaring brightness of the crowded street. "Is he still out there?"

Maggie turned to look. "I . . . don't know." She hated lying like this. She was amazed that she could come up with a story so quickly with those disturbing brown eyes gazing at her. But there was no way she could tell him the truth.

"Well, just in case he's still watching . . ." Charles leaned forward and kissed her.

He kissed her.

On the mouth.

His lips were warm and soft and he tasted like lemonade.

Maggie was caught so off guard, she could do nothing but laugh.

He laughed too.

His smile was incredible, and Maggie realized she'd never truly seen Chuck smile. Sure, he'd made an attempt. He'd twisted his lips in a vague imitation, but it had been nothing like this. Something had happened over the past seven years to make him forget how.

"Maybe we better do that again," he suggested, his grin widening. "Make sure this man—whoever he is— really gets the message."

Charles started to lean forward again, and whether he was only teasing or not, Maggie would never know, because temporary insanity overcame her and she leaned forward, too, closing the gap between them.

And then he was kissing her again. Not a swift gentle brushing of lips like the last kiss, but a longer, deeper kiss. Maggie felt a jolt of disbelief as his tongue swept into her mouth. Not disbelief that he would kiss her that way, but that she would welcome such a kiss, that she would kiss him back with such abandon, and most of all, that she wanted that kiss to go on and on and on.

Forever.

It had to be insanity—she'd never do something like kiss a total stranger without having first lost her mind. Except he wasn't a total stranger. He was so much like Chuck. A Chuck who still remembered how to smile and laugh.

"Well," Charles breathed as he pulled back to look into her eyes. "Yeah. That was pretty damn territorial. I think if the man who was following you was watching that, he's probably convinced that you're not single and . . . are you, by any chance, single?"

His eyes were filled with a molten heat. Maggie had seen traces of the same fire in Chuck's eyes, but Chuck was quick to try to hide it, while Charles had no qualms against letting her see his attraction.

She cleared her throat as she straightened up, gently freeing herself from his grasp. "Yeah," she said, having some trouble catching her breath. "Yes, I sort of am. Single."

Chuck had told her that the physical attraction between them had been instant when they met. He hadn't been kidding.

Charles picked up on her evasive wording. "Sort of?"

There was no way she could explain that over the past day or so she had been fighting the totally insane urge to have a love affair with the man he would become in seven years. Fortunately, he let it go.

"Do you have a name?" he asked.

"Maggie," she told him.

"Maggie," he repeated. The way he said it, it sounded like a caress.

"Winthrop," she said, moistening her suddenly dry lips with the tip of her tongue. "Maggie Winthrop."

Charles held out his hand. "Pleased to meet you, Maggie Winthrop."

His hand was big and warm, with long, graceful fingers. Instead of shaking her hand as she expected, he lifted her fingers to his lips and kissed the back of her hand.

Maggie had to laugh again. Again, from knowing the grim and seemingly dangerous man he would become, she never would have dreamed he could be so utterly flirtatious. And smooth. He was *very* smooth, as if he'd had a great amount of practice using his considerable charms to seduce. And his charms were considerable, as he darn well knew. He didn't let go of her hand as he smiled at her again.

"I'm Charles—"

"Della Croce," she finished for him. "I know."

He froze for just a fraction of a second. "You do?"

"You work over at Data Tech," she explained. "I do too. Sort of."

He released her hand. "There's that 'sort of' again."

"I'm a freelance writer. I just signed a contract with Data Tech to do a couple of projects including the annual report. I'll be in and out over the next few months until all the jobs are complete."

He shifted in his seat, his gaze intense, sharp with curiosity and a hint of wariness. "As far as I know, I've got nothing to do with the annual report. What made you recognize me?"

"I've seen you around. That, combined with gossip heard at the coffee machine . . ." Maggie lied again. Still, this one wasn't a very big lie. She had no doubt that this man was talked about frequently as the women in the office took their morning coffee break.

He laughed. "If it's gossip, it's probably not true."

He was still gazing at her, and despite the warmth in his eyes, she was struck by his coolness, his reserve. It was odd, really. There was heat in his eyes—heat from desire and attraction. But at the same time he held himself aloof, keeping himself emotionally distanced.

Maggie had seen that same distance in Chuck, she realized, but it wasn't as glaringly obvious. With Chuck, it was hidden beneath his burning anger. It was dwarfed by his desperate need to set things right.

In a burst of nervous energy so much like Chuck's, Charles drummed his fingers on the table for the briefest of moments before forcing himself to stop. It was a gesture so like Chuck's because Charles *was* Chuck. Or rather, at one time, Chuck had been Charles.

"You called me Chuck," he remembered suddenly. "When you first sat down."

"I knew your name was Charles, I assumed Chuck was a nickname."

"I don't have a nickname. I've just always been Charles."

"Even when you were a child?"

Something shifted in his eyes, and Maggie got the impression of a drawbridge being raised and clanging shut with a metallic thud against the very private outer defenses of an impenetrable castle. "No," he said. "Not even when I was a child."

"No nicknames, huh? None at all?" she asked. "Come on. There must be something." She wanted to rock the foundations of that castle. "What do women call you when you take them to bed?"

For one short moment Charles dropped his guard, and Maggie could see honest emotion in his eyes. Surprise, and genuine amusement. But then heat sparked, drowning out all else. "I don't know," he murmured. "Want to try it and see?"

She was treading upon extremely dangerous territory.

Still she couldn't forget what Chuck had told her. She'd dated this deliciously sexy man, and because he wouldn't share more than the physical with her, she'd kept their relationship from becoming intimate.

She still wanted more from him.

"Can I talk you into having lunch with me?" he asked.

Maggie shook her head no, glancing at her watch. "I have to go. I have a one o'clock meeting." But instead of standing up, she leaned forward. "Charles, tell me something. Tell me just one thing about yourself that you've never told anyone before."

He hesitated just long enough so that for a moment Maggie thought he might actually do it.

But he didn't. "I hate carrot cake," he said.

She laughed to cover her disappointment. "The fact that you hate carrot cake is a deeply personal secret?"

"Actually, yes, it is."

Maggie shook her head in despair as she stood up. "Thanks for . . . helping me."

He rose to his feet, and once again she was struck by his height. "Wait—"

She started for the door. "I really have to go."

"Without giving me your phone number? I'd like to see you again, Maggie."

She turned and looked up at Charles Della Croce. "Oh, you'll see me again," she told him. "You can count on it."

FOUR

Maggie got to the mall at seven-thirty.

Chuck had left a message on her answering machine, asking her to meet him there at six, but she'd had a dinner meeting scheduled with a client. It was a meeting that she couldn't get out of. Or maybe she simply didn't *want* to get out of it. Maybe she was intentionally trying to keep her distance from this man.

Lord knows she'd let herself get a little too close to Charles this afternoon.

As Maggie hurried into the air-conditioned coolness of the shopping mall, she wondered if Chuck would still be waiting for her. She hadn't had any way to contact him to tell him about her meeting, and he hadn't called back.

He was sitting on one of the benches near the movie theater, reading a book, just the way he'd said he'd be. Maggie felt a surge of emotion at the sight of him. It may have been relief. Or it may have been something else entirely.

He stood up as she approached.

"Sorry I'm so late," she told him. "I had a meeting that couldn't be rescheduled."

"I figured it was something like that," he said. "Did you eat?"

"Yeah. Did you?" Why was she so nervous? Just standing here talking to him, saying nothing of any importance whatsoever, was making her feel totally on edge.

"I grabbed something from the food court about a half hour ago."

Maybe it was the way he was looking at her, with his usual high-powered intensity. It was as if he were memorizing every detail of her—face, clothes, hair, everything. And all *she* could think about was that he was surely noticing every wrinkle in her denim skirt, every chip in the polish on her toenails, every scuff mark in the leather of her sandals.

"Come on," he said, slipping his book into the back pocket of his jeans. "There's something I want you to try on."

Maggie had to laugh. "Are you kidding? We're here to go *shopping*?"

One side of his mouth turned up in wry half smile. "You don't think I asked you to meet me at the mall simply for the atmosphere, do you?"

"Actually, I didn't think about it," Maggie admitted, hurrying to keep up.

"We're here to buy you a dress to wear to the Data Tech party."

Maggie stopped short. "I don't need a dress. I've already figured out what I'm going to wear—"

"Black pants with a tuxedo-style jacket," Chuck told her, "over a shirt made of some kind of shimmery material."

"Yeah," she said slowly. "That's what I'm going to wear. It's formal without being too feminine. It's businesslike. It's not too . . ."

"Sexy?" he supplied.

Maggie lifted her chin. "That's right. In order to compete in the male-dominated world of business, women have to be careful not to—"

"I happen to think it made you look incredibly sexy."

Maggie started walking again, trying to hide the way his softly spoken words affected her. "Then why are we buying me a new dress?"

Chuck glanced at her. "Because over the past seven years there's been a time or two when you went all out and got really dressed up and wore a . . . I don't know, maybe you'd call it a gown. It was some kind of really fancy dress and you wore your hair up and . . ." And each time he had seen her dressed like that, it had damn near stopped his heart.

But he couldn't tell her that.

"Just trust me on this, all right?" he said.

She was silent, walking alongside him, carefully not meeting his eyes. Trust him, Chuck had told her. But he wouldn't blame her one bit if she didn't trust him. After all, in her mind he'd given her nothing of himself, nothing to make her think that he trusted her in return.

In her mind.

In truth, he had. In truth, he'd told her something he'd never told anyone before.

"Carrot cake," he said.

She stopped in front of a shoe store's window display to stare at him. "Excuse me?"

"The fact that I don't like carrot cake really was something I'd never told anyone." He could see surprise and confusion in her eyes, so he tried to explain as he pulled her closer to the window, out of the stream of pedestrian traffic. "When I was little, I went to live with my uncle, my mother's brother, and his housekeeper made me a carrot cake the first day I arrived. I really hated it, I mean, *hated* it—but I ate it because it seemed rude not to."

Maggie was still staring at him, her eyes wide.

Chuck cleared his throat. "I, um, I guess, you know, because I didn't want to be there, I had this sense that everything was destined to be awful, but I was stuck there until I was old enough to live on my own. I don't know, it seemed kind of appropriate that I choke down that terrible cake. So I did, and Jen, the housekeeper, got it into her head that I really loved her carrot cake, so she made it for me all the time. Every holiday, every birthday. She'd probably still be making it for me now, but my uncle finally died a few years ago, and she retired."

Maggie didn't say a word.

"I know I didn't manage to get that all out this morning, but that's what I was talking about when I told you that I hated carrot cake," Chuck told her.

"This morning . . ." The surprise in Maggie's eyes turned to suspicion. "Did you follow me today? Oh, my

God. Did you somehow listen in on my conversation with Charles?"

Chuck had to laugh. It started as a chuckle but grew into a full laugh. He couldn't remember the last time he'd laughed this way. "Mags. You don't get it, do you? Think about it. Think about what you just said."

But her expression had changed again. She was looking at him now much the way she'd looked at him this morning. This morning, in her time. Seven years of mornings earlier in his.

He could see his own attraction for her mirrored in her eyes. And he could see something else, something warm and soft, something that made him nearly dizzy with longing.

"You don't do that often enough," Maggie told him quietly. "You don't laugh anymore. Or even smile."

She reached out then, gently touching the side of his face, and he remembered the heaven it had been to kiss her. Seven years ago she'd walked into that restaurant in downtown Scottsdale. He was supposed to meet Boyd Rogers for lunch, but Boyd had called and canceled. And then Maggie had appeared, telling him some ridiculous story about someone following her. He'd been so enchanted by her sparkling smile, by the way she seemed to look at him with something akin to wonder in her eyes, he hadn't been able to resist. He'd kissed her. Twice. God, he could remember the softness of her lips, the sweetness of her mouth as if it were yesterday.

Or more precisely, as if it were about eleven forty-five this morning.

"I didn't follow you," he told her. "I didn't have to. I was there." He saw the realization dawn in her eyes, and he said aloud the words she already knew. "I was there, because I'm Charles. Or rather, I *was* Charles."

He'd spent most of the day going to movies. It had taken him almost no time to find the perfect dress for Maggie to wear to the Data Tech holiday party, and then he'd had the entire rest of the day free.

He'd walked around the mall for a bit, delighting in his ability to take his time, to stroll without his crowd of bodyguards hurrying him along. It had been years since his experiments with time travel had been made public knowledge. And after that, as a target for terrorists and lunatics, he'd needed professional protection. He'd taken the time to learn to protect himself as well, and there was still a part of him that constantly checked in the glass windows and mirrors of the mall stores to make sure he wasn't being followed.

But of course he wasn't being followed. In this year, in this time, no one gave a damn about Dr. Charles Della Croce. He liked it that way.

That morning, he'd bought a ticket to the eleven-thirty showing of a movie whose name he couldn't even remember now, and halfway through he'd been flooded with memories—new memories, double memories—of meeting Maggie Winthrop for the first time not at the Data Tech party, but rather at a little restaurant in Scottsdale.

The memory was fuzzy at first, and he really had to work to recall the incident. Even then, it didn't seem to gel until he remembered that kiss. Somehow that sweet sensation brought the entire encounter into sharp focus. Then he remembered the conversation he and Maggie had had almost word for word.

He hadn't bothered to watch the rest of the movie. He'd spent the time instead sitting there in the darkened theater with his eyes closed, replaying that second incredible kiss over and over in his mind, trying to make that memory stronger, willing himself to recall something that had happened seven years ago.

Something that had happened mere moments before.

But now Maggie was here, inches away from him, and he didn't have to rely on memories. Her gaze flicked down to his mouth before she looked searchingly into his eyes. She smiled then, very slightly, and he knew she was thinking about that incredible kiss too.

"That *was* you, wasn't it?" she whispered.

Chuck nodded. "Yeah. That was me."

Maggie held her breath, entranced by the way, once again, just like this morning, he took his time leaning closer and closer until his mouth covered hers. He kissed her, slowly, sweetly, almost reverently.

Then he reached for her, pulling her tightly against him, burying his face in her hair as he held her close. "I've been dying to do that again for the past seven years."

"Chuck—" Maggie lifted her head to look up at him, but instantly forgot whatever it was she'd intended to say. The heat in his eyes seemed to magnify all of the secrets revealed by the intimacy of their embrace. He wanted her. Badly. She couldn't help but know that.

And when he lowered his head to kiss her again, she kissed him back hungrily, desperately, reaching up to meet him on the tips of her toes. She pulled him even more tightly against her, running her fingers through the nearly unbearable softness of his hair. All of her senses seemed to explode as she kissed him harder, deeper, as if all of the emotions of the past few days stood up in unison and cried out to be heard.

Heard and harkened to.

Maggie had had complete sexual encounters that were far less powerful, and far less meaningful, than this single kiss.

He pulled back, pushing her away to arm's length, breathing hard, both alarm and elation written clearly on his face, as if he had been able to follow her very thoughts.

"Dear God," he breathed.

As Maggie gazed into his eyes she knew that with that kiss, she had given far too much away—she had revealed way too much of her feelings. She took no comfort from knowing that Chuck had done the same.

"That was a mistake," he told her.

She pulled free from his grasp so that he wouldn't see the disappointment she knew was on her face. "Yeah," she said. "You're probably right. A big mistake."

He *was* right. What was she thinking? What was she doing?

The last thing in the world she needed was to get involved with a man who took seven years to open up and tell her why he hated carrot cake. "Let's find that dress and get out of here."

"How's this?" Maggie's voice interrupted Chuck's reverie, and he turned to see her standing in The Dress.

It was the one. He'd known from the moment he saw it on the mannequin in the store. He would have bought it right there and then, at quarter past ten that morning, but when it came to women's clothing sizes, he was clueless. A fourteen seemed much too big, and a four was surely too tiny. Maggie was somewhere in between the two, but where, Chuck couldn't begin to guess.

"Please don't look at me like that," she said tightly. "It's making me nervous."

"I'm not sure I can be in the same room with you and *not* look at you like this," he admitted. "You look . . . amazing."

She'd pulled her hair up off her neck, holding it in place with one of those bear-trap-like clip things that she'd no doubt had in her purse. Several tendrils had escaped, hanging down around her shoulders, accentuating the sheer elegance of the strapless gown.

The dress itself was a rich shade of brown, made of some kind of fabric that managed to be both velvety and silky. It clung intimately to the soft curves of her breasts, yet fell smoothly, gracefully across her stomach and hips, cascading all the way down to her ankles.

It had a neckline that was shaped with the swell of her body, dipping down to meet between her breasts. And it had a slit up the side, all the way to her thighs. He couldn't tell it was there now, while she was standing still, but when she moved, he knew it would reveal tantalizing glimpses of her legs.

She turned away, going back into the changing room.

Chuck could see himself reflected in the store mirror. From a distance, he looked the same as he ever did, nearly the same as he did seven years ago. But he wasn't the same. The road he'd taken over the past years had been a rough one, fueled by his obsession to find a way back to the past.

He'd sold his soul for the chance to develop and test his theories. He'd danced with the devil that was Wizard-9, and soon he was going to have to pay the ultimate price.

Maggie came out into the store, dressed once again in her sleeveless blouse and denim skirt, the dress on a hanger, the long skirt looped over her arm. She didn't do more than glance at him, as if she were afraid to meet his eyes, and Chuck knew that his talk of mistakes had hurt her.

But it was true. Getting involved with him—physically or otherwise—was surely the last thing she needed.

Chuck followed her over to the cash register and took the dress from her. She wandered around the front of the store as he used cash to pay, as the store clerk wrapped the dress in tissue paper and put it into a shopping bag with handles.

Maggie looked up as he headed toward her, and together they left the store.

"My car's over by Sears," she told him. "On the lower level."

They walked for a moment in silence, and then, as if she couldn't stand it another moment, Maggie spoke. "You know, it *wasn't* a mistake."

She was talking about that kiss. "Yes, it was," he said gently.

"Why?"

Chuck had to close his eyes briefly at the impossible irony. He'd wanted this woman for years. *Years.* He'd kept his distance when she dated and then married Albert Ford, but he'd never stopped wanting her. If anything, the years and their continued friendship had made him want her more. Yet now here he was, about to talk her out of the kind of relationship he'd ever only dreamed of having.

"Because I need you to help me change *Charles*'s future."

She forcefully pushed open the door and he followed her out into the warm night air. "But you're Charles, and Charles is *you*," she argued.

Yes, he was Charles, but Charles wasn't him. Charles hadn't made the mistakes that he'd made. Charles hadn't put an entire nation in jeopardy. Charles hadn't been tainted by his connection to Wizard-9.

"Here's what I think we should do," Chuck said to Maggie as they crossed the car-filled parking lot. "You take this dress and go home, and tomorrow night wear it over to Data Tech and . . ."

Chuck had seen the car approaching the moment they exited the mall. He'd been watching it out of the corner of one eye, his wariness a habit that was impossible to break. The car was moving too fast, bouncing jarringly over the speed bumps. But it was the fact that the windows were tinted and the front passenger's window—the side nearest them—was rolled slightly down that made the hair stand up on the back of his neck.

He was reacting even before he saw the slight movement at the window, even before his mind registered the fact that that was, indeed, the barrel of a gun being aimed at them.

He caught Maggie around the waist, pulling her down between two cars, dragging her to cover as an assault rifle was fired from the open window of the car. Bullets slammed into the cars around them, breaking windows and tearing into the metal with a terrible screeching sound.

And as quickly as it had started, it was over. The car was speeding away with a squeal of tires.

The explosive racket of a weapon being fired at close range still rang in Chuck's ears as he took one shaky breath and then another. He realized he had thrown himself on top of Maggie in a ludicrous attempt to shield her from the bullets with his body. He was probably crushing her, grinding her into the rough asphalt. But she didn't move beneath him, didn't protest, didn't make a sound.

A drowning wave of panic washed over him as he pushed himself off of her, terrified that the future was repeating itself. *Please God, don't let her have been hit. . . .*

But Maggie moved then, throwing her arms around his neck and clinging tightly to him. She was alive. His relief nearly knocked him over, and as he sat up he pulled her with him, cradling her in his arms. He ran his hands over her, reassuring himself that with the exception of a slightly skinned knee, she was all right.

She seemed only to want to hold him tightly. He could feel her trembling, or maybe that was him, he wasn't sure anymore. But then, God, she lifted her face, and just like that, he was kissing her. Kissing her as if the world were coming to an end.

In some ways, it was.

This was what he should have wanted more than anything else in the world. Maggie, with all of her passion and joy and those smart-aleck comments that always made him smile. Maggie, with her million-watt grin, her husky laugh, and her sparkling eyes. Maggie, not just his best friend, but the keeper of his heart and soul—his lover, his only, his wife.

If only he had fought as hard for her as he'd fought to develop his theories on time travel . . .

But *what ifs* weren't any use to him now. Chuck had come too far down his own path ever to turn back. But Charles, Charles still had a chance to choose heaven over hell.

Only Chuck was finding out firsthand just how very hard it was to let go once he held heaven in his arms.

Especially since heaven was responding to each kiss he gave her with a fierceness and intensity that damn near took his breath away. She wanted him as badly as he wanted her. Chuck couldn't stop his feelings of elation. He wanted to sing, to dance dizzily with her in circles, spinning and jumping and whirling like crazy until they fell, laughing, together on the ground.

But what he had to do instead was stop kissing her.

It took everything Chuck had in him to pull back. And even then, it was only the fact that they were in danger that made him stop.

"We have to get out of here." His voice sounded hoarse.

"We can go to my place." He could hear her desire in her voice, see it in her eyes. God, she thought he was talking about . . .

"I mean, we can if you want," she added more softly, almost uncertainly.

I want, he wanted to tell her. *God, do I want.* . . .

"No, Mags," he said instead, "I meant whoever did this might come back. And if they do, I want us far from here."

"Who *was* that? Who would shoot at *us*?" Maggie started to get up, but he grabbed her wrist and kept her down, her head lower than the hoods of the cars surrounding them.

As Chuck got to his feet he stayed in a crouch, too, reaching around the car to grab the bag that he'd dropped. "Not us—me." Taking her hand and staying low to the ground, he started moving between the cars.

"But why?"

She figured it out herself, and as he answered they spoke in unison. "The Wells Project."

She was quick to add, "You said the men from Wizard-9 didn't follow you here. You said they couldn't."

"I didn't think they could. I *know* I disabled the prototype." Chuck frowned. "I also know they destroyed my lab at Data Tech. I assumed the working model of the Runabout and the other equipment were in there at the time." He glanced back at her. "And you know that old saying about the word *assume*."

"You mean, when you assume, you and me get a bullet in the ass?"

Chuck had to laugh. Somehow the direst, most serious thing that could have happened *had* happened. Wizard-9 agents had followed him into the past, using techniques he himself had written about to find him. The ripple effect. Or the displacement theory. It was possible to trace the Runabout as it traveled through time using either of those theories. Neither was one hundred percent accurate, but obviously Wizard-9 had been close enough.

But despite the danger, Maggie had still managed to make him laugh.

Still, the situation was extremely sobering. The latest working model of the Runabout could hold four travelers for each leap in time. The technology was still in its early stages, and for the first time since the Wells Project went on-line, Chuck was grateful for that. Even in this advanced version of the Runabout, the energy source required at least ninety-six hours for its various components to cool and reset before another jump through time could be made.

He had to figure it had taken the Wizard-9 agents a full twenty-four hours to track him here to the mall. It had probably taken them a whole lot less than that, but he estimated high just to be safe.

That left him only seventy-two hours. After seventy-two hours, he'd be a dead man. After seventy-two hours, Wizard-9 would be able to make another leap through time. This time, they'd arrive before him, and when he made the jump, when he arrived naked and disoriented in Maggie's backyard, they'd be there waiting. And they'd kill him.

Maggie tugged on his hand. "My car's over this way."

He shook his head. Seventy-two hours. God, the clock was ticking. "We can't risk taking it. If this *is* Wizard-9, then they've already found your car and rigged it with some kind of tracking device. Or a bomb."

"A bomb!" Even Maggie couldn't make a joke about that. "Like . . . a *bomb*?"

"A bomb," Chuck told her. "Like the one they planted that took out most of the White House, and all of the presidential staff down to and including the Speaker of the House."

"If they could find my car in this parking lot, then they've surely found my house," Maggie said.

"That's right," Chuck said, moving down the line of parked cars, looking quickly at each one they passed. "We can't go there."

"Where are we going to go?" Maggie asked. "An even bigger question: if we can't take my car, how are we going to get there? Wherever *there* is."

He glanced back at her. "We'll have to borrow someone else's car."

Maggie dug in her heels. "*Borrow* someone else's car? It's not as if we're going to find one with the keys in the ignition," she said. "What are you going to do? Hot-wire it?"

Chuck nodded. "Absolutely."

FIVE

"I can't believe you know how to hot-wire a car."

Chuck glanced away from the road and over at Maggie, his face dimly lit by the green dashboard light. "It's all a matter of understanding how things work."

It was obvious to Maggie from the ease with which Chuck had started the engine of this white, late-model Taurus with only the Swiss army knife he had in his pocket, that he had a clear understanding of how things worked.

It was obvious, too, that he had an understanding of how to *keep* things working when he not only switched license plates with the car next to the white Taurus, but stopped in another badly lit corner of the parking lot and quickly switched plates a third time.

It was likely that while someone coming out of the mall would notice that their car was missing, they probably wouldn't notice that their plates had been switched. And while the state police would be on the lookout for a white Taurus with the original plates, they wouldn't be looking for a white Taurus with this third set of plates.

Chuck glanced at her again, and Maggie realized she was staring at him, but she couldn't seem to stop. His face looked angular in the shadows, his cheekbones in sharp relief.

There was more than mere age that made him look different than Charles. There was a hardness to his mouth, an edge to him that made her wonder with a shiver just where he'd draw the line in his quest to set things right.

They were traveling north on Route 17, heading up into the mountains, toward Sedona and Flagstaff. The tires of the car made a low humming sound on the highway as they moved at a speed slightly over the limit.

They'd made only one stop—right before they left the city limits. Chuck had pulled up to a roadhouse-style bar, and he and Maggie had gone inside.

They weren't there to quench their thirst. No, in just a matter of minutes after walking into the place, they were seated at a table in the back, across from a man who looked as if he hadn't bathed since Jimmy Carter was in office. As Maggie incredulously looked on, Chuck paid a hundred and fifty dollars cash for a deadly-looking handgun, a shoulder holster, and a box of ammunition.

The two men shook hands, and then—cool as a cucumber, as if he wore an illegally obtained, unregistered handgun underneath his jacket all the time—Chuck slipped the leather straps on over his shirt. Somehow he knew how to fasten it all together to make it work as a holster. He checked the gun—for what, Maggie didn't know; to see if it was loaded?—then slipped it into the holster, putting his jacket back on to hide it. The box of bullets went into his pocket.

Maggie didn't say a thing.

Chuck suggested they make use of the facilities before they hit the road again, and when she came out of the ladies' room, he was talking on the pay phone. He hung up as she approached. He didn't tell her whom he'd called, and she didn't ask.

She didn't say a word as they walked back out to their stolen car. She still didn't speak as once more he used his knowledge of how things worked to restart the Taurus.

Now, though, she cleared her throat. "Where are we going?"

Chuck glanced at her. "Maybe you should close your eyes, try to get some sleep. We've got a long night ahead of us."

"Yeah, right. I always get the urge to take a nap after nearly being gunned down at the mall."

He looked at her again, longer this time. "I'm sorry," he said. "I'm sorry I got you involved in this. I should have stayed far away from you. If I'd been thinking straight, I would have realized that Ken Goodwin would never let something like the Wells Project be destroyed."

"Ken Goodwin?"

"Out of all the Wizard-9 agents I dealt with, he seemed to be the one in charge. If he's here, if he's behind this . . ."

"What?" Maggie prompted softly. "Talk to me."

His eyes seemed to flash as he shot her another quick look. "This whole situation has just gone from difficult to near impossible. Goodwin knows that I need to get close to Charles to keep him from developing those time-travel theories."

"Charles!" Maggie said suddenly, turning in her seat to face him. "Wizard-9 can get to you through Charles. If they kill him, you'll be dead too."

"No, that's not a problem."

"But the way you explained it to me—"

"They won't risk hurting Charles," Chuck reassured her. "They need him alive to develop the time-travel theory. My bet is they won't even get near him, for fear of interfering with the natural course of events. No, *I'm* the one Goodwin needs to get rid of. If I get within fifty feet of Charles, Wizard-9 is going to be there to stop me cold."

"What about me?" Maggie asked. "I could approach Charles—"

"No. They'll be looking for you too. They know who you are. They know what you did in the future."

She studied his profile. "What exactly did I do?"

Chuck was silent, his eyes fixed on the road ahead of him. When he finally spoke, his voice was almost unnaturally matter-of-fact. "I told you what you did. You warned me. You saved my life."

"How?"

He shifted slightly, impatiently in his seat, glancing briefly at her. "You said, 'Chuck, look out!' You know, Mags, when we're talking, I can't think, I can't plan. I need to think this through and figure out what Goodwin would expect me to do. And then I need to figure out if I should do that, or do the opposite, depending on whether or not he'd expect me to second-guess him and—"

"Okay, okay! You've convinced me. I'll shut up." Maggie's voice shook very slightly as she added, "I'm sorry."

"No." Chuck's voice was barely audible over the hum of the engine. "*I'm* sorry. I'm sorry for getting you into this. And I'm sorry I can't be the man you need me to be."

Maggie reached out, lightly touching his denim-clad leg. "I think if we want to stay alive—and I don't know about you, but I sure do—you're exactly the man I need you to be."

Chuck didn't say anything. He didn't even look at her. But he did take her hand, intertwining their fingers.

They headed north into the Arizona night in silence, holding tightly to one another's hand.

They had to walk from the bus station to the motel in the early-morning sunshine. It wasn't more than a few blocks, but to Maggie, it seemed like a thousand miles. It had been years since she'd pulled an all-nighter like this one.

They'd left the stolen car at the Flagstaff airport and had taken a shuttle across town to the bus station. They'd had to wait nearly three hours for the next bus heading back to Phoenix.

As they'd snacked on candy and cans of sodas from the vending machines in the bus station, Chuck had explained why they were heading back south—doubling back on their six, as he called it.

They had to return to Phoenix because Charles was there, because he was the key to changing Maggie's future and Chuck's past. Ken Goodwin and his agents from Wizard-9 would expect them to return, but Chuck was banking on the fact that Wizard-9 wouldn't be ready for them to return this soon. Over the course of the next twenty-four hours Wizard-9 would set up roadblocks and spot inspections on the routes leading into the city in an attempt to intercept them.

But by then, Chuck and Maggie would have already returned to Phoenix.

Maggie had pointed out that it was possible Wizard-9 was as adrift and as out of place as Chuck was in this time frame. Maybe they wouldn't have the resources or connections needed to authorize the setting up of roadblocks. But despite their botched assassination attempt, Chuck seemed to think they were capable of anything.

He was determined to return to Phoenix as soon as possible.

The stolen car was left in the airport as a false lead. When they found it, the agents from Wizard-9 would waste valuable time and manpower attempting to pick up Chuck and Maggie's trail in the Flagstaff area.

But their trail would long be cold.

Chuck had briefly considered leaving Maggie safely hidden up in the mountains. But Maggie didn't even have time to protest before he told her he'd rejected that idea flat out. Apparently, where Wizard-9 was concerned, there was no such thing as *safely* hidden. The only way Chuck could guarantee her safety was if he was with her.

It was also there, in the late-night quiet of the Flag-staff bus station, that Chuck had told her that kiss they'd shared in the mall parking lot had been another mistake.

The clock on the wall of the motel lobby said 8:30 A.M. as Maggie watched Chuck fill out the motel registration form. He paid in cash, and a few minutes later they unlocked the door to a room.

One room.

A single, solitary room.

Chuck entered first, tossing the bag with the dress in it onto one of the two double beds before he turned to switch on the heater. The November night had been cold and a chill lingered in the room.

Maggie stood in the doorway as the old machine underneath the front window wheezed to life. "I don't think this is a good idea."

He knew she was talking about the fact that he'd gotten only one room. "I need to know that you're safe. There're two beds." He switched the heater on high, turning the knob to the warmest setting, then straightened up. "Come in and close the door. You're drawing attention to us."

Maggie stepped inside, leaning back against the door to shut it.

Two beds. He was right. There were two beds. But as far as Maggie could tell, there wasn't a brick wall with a steel-reinforced, heavily padlocked door separating them.

"I won't touch you," he continued, glancing at her in the dim light of the lamps. His face was grim, his mouth a tight line. "I promise."

It wasn't the idea of Chuck losing control that Maggie was afraid of. It was her own inability to stay away from him that frightened her. So far she'd failed rather miserably in her attempts to keep her distance from this man. Chuck may have been sure that the kisses they'd shared had been mistakes, but to Maggie they had felt impossibly right. He may have been sure, but she wasn't at all certain she was strong enough to fight her attraction to him much longer.

She cleared her throat. "I'm just . . ." A deep breath and then she started again. "We've been together constantly all night. No offense, but I could really use some time away from you and—"

"No." He crossed to the sink that was on the wall outside of the bathroom and began washing the miles of travel off his hands and face. He met her eyes in the mirror. "I'm sorry. If we need to leave out the back window, we can be gone in a matter of seconds. But if you're in another room, even next door . . ." He shook his head. "We're toast."

The high window in back of the little room was not easy to access, but Maggie had no doubt that Chuck could get it opened if they needed to leave in a hurry. He was proving to be something of an expert at all kinds of unexpected things.

"What kind of scientist who works in an R and D lab knows how to get hold of a gun and hot-wire a car?" she asked. "Where did you learn things like 'doubling back on our six,' or whatever you called it?" She paused. "Isn't that some kind of military expression?"

"Yeah." Chuck dried his face with a hand towel, still watching her in the mirror. "You can pinpoint locations by using the numbers from the face of a clock." He pointed directly to his right. "The bathroom door is at three o'clock. The sink is at twelve. Right now you're standing at my seven—"

"And directly behind you—where you've already been before—is your six."

He gave her a slight smile. "Right."

"So, what, did you learn that in the Data Tech employees' manual or something?"

"Or something."

Maggie sat down on one of the beds. The mattress was soft and springy. Sitting down felt good, though. And lying down would feel even better. She sank down onto her back, her feet still on the floor as she stared up at the cracks in the motel-room ceiling. "Would it really kill you to be more specific?"

She heard the creak as Chuck sat down on the other bed, heard the double thuds as he took off his boots and tossed them onto the floor.

She was actually surprised when he finally spoke.

"Shortly after the news leaked out that I was working on the Wells Project, I started getting death threats. Some were just threats, but some were real. A few were near misses. At the time I had a friend who was thinking about retiring from the Navy. He was in the SEAL units, and he had some . . . skills that I thought would come in handy. I hired him as a security consultant. He taught me a bunch of nifty little tricks."

"Where was he when the Wizard-9 agents tried to ambush you in your lab?"

Chuck didn't answer right away, and Maggie turned her head to look at him.

He was still sitting on the edge of the other bed. His

feet were bare, and his elbows were resting on his knees, his shoulders bent with fatigue. Or despair. He was resting his forehead in the palm of one hand, rubbing it slightly as if he had a headache. But he glanced up as if he felt her gaze on him.

"He was dead," he answered. "They shot him in the back of the head at close range before I got to the lab that morning." He paused. "You saw them do it."

Maggie's breath caught in her throat. "Oh my God."

He looked away from her, breaking the almost palpable connection that had shimmered between them. "I'm sorry. I shouldn't have told you that."

Maggie sat up. "No," she said. "Chuck, I want you to talk to me. I wish you would tell me *more.*"

He stood up. "We should get to sleep."

Maggie felt a surge of frustration. Why wouldn't he talk to her? She could see his pain etched into the lines of his face. He tried to hide it, tried to pretend it didn't matter. Nothing mattered but fixing the mistake he'd made.

But the desperation and anguish of the wild-eyed man who'd first pounded on her back door was not gone. All those emotions were still inside of him, despite being carefully locked away. He worked hard to stay in control, never to lose sight of his single goal.

His control had slipped only when he'd given in to passion. He'd dropped his guard only when he'd kissed her. He'd kissed her as if there could be no secrets between them, as if their hearts beat in perfect unison, as if they were two parts of a single whole.

But those kisses were wrong, or so Chuck said when

he'd regained his precious control. They were mistakes that weren't meant to happen.

Maggie fought the frustration that rose up into her throat, choking her. Across the room, Chuck unwrapped the dress they had bought at the mall.

The mall. Maggie nearly laughed aloud. It had been hardly more than twelve hours since she'd met him outside of the movie theater. It had been hardly more than twelve hours since her life had been forever and irrevocably changed. But what had changed it most? The rain of bullets that had very nearly taken her life? Or that incredible, soul-shattering, heart-stopping kiss she'd shared with Chuck immediately after?

When Chuck had kissed her, she thought she'd found all of the answers she'd ever been searching for. But Chuck had only found that he'd made a mistake.

As he carefully hung the dress on a hanger, the fabric glistened in the dim light, an odd spot of elegance in the shabby room.

"Why bother?" she asked. Her voice sounded harsh in the stillness.

He turned to look at her, and she held his gaze pointedly, almost aggressively, as if daring him to look away from her.

He didn't look away, but his eyes revealed nothing of what he was feeling. "Why bother hanging this up?" he asked.

"Yeah. I'm not going to be able to go to the party tomorrow night—no, *tonight*. The party's tonight." Everything was happening so fast. Maggie took a deep breath. "If the guys in Wizard-9 are so smart, it won't be long before they notice that my name is on the guest list—"

"I'm sure they already know," Chuck told her. "And you're right. The party's no longer an option. But you can still wear the dress. I just have to figure out an alternative time and place for you and Charles to meet."

He spoke so quietly, so matter-of-factly, as if nothing about this insanity affected him personally. Well, shoot, maybe it didn't. *He* wasn't the one who was going to have to get all dressed up in a ludicrous attempt to catch the attention of a man she knew damn well wasn't interested—the seven-years-younger version of a man who had told her their kisses had been a mistake.

"I don't know how you think I'm ever going to be able to talk Charles into something as huge as changing his career." Her voice shook, but she couldn't help it. She didn't care, anyway. She had every right to be upset, dammit. She'd been shot at and dragged halfway across the state and back all in one night. She'd found everything she'd ever wanted, only to realize she hadn't found anything at all. Because the kind of love she wanted was a love that was returned.

"Just be yourself. He won't be able to resist you."

She rose to her feet as her temper blazed. "Resist what? What exactly is it you want me to do, Chuck?"

But he wasn't going to let her fight with him. He turned away, pulling back the covers of his bed. "Let's just go to sleep. It's been a long night."

He was so calm, so cool. Maggie wanted to see beneath his facade. She wanted to get a rise out of him. She wanted to see *some*thing in him besides this grim determination. "You want me to sleep with him, right? Okay.

You win. I'll do it. But I have to warn you. If I have sex with Charles, you'll have a memory of it too."

He stood quietly, expressionlessly. "Maggie, this isn't about sex."

"If it wasn't about sex, you wouldn't've cared if I wore a potato sack the next time I met Charles," she countered hotly, gesturing toward the dress hanging in the corner. "And *that's* no potato sack."

"You're right. It's about sex." His lack of emotion was driving her crazy. "But not entirely. It's more complicated than that."

"Complicated is putting it mildly." Her voice cracked. "I don't know why you think I have the power to make Charles change his entire life. You tell me he won't be able to resist me. But, hey! *You* have no problem resisting me. All you do is push me away—"

Chuck turned away with a forceful exhale of air halfway between laughter and a sob. And just like that, he wasn't standing still anymore. He was moving, using one hand to rake back his unruly hair as he paced toward the sink.

Maggie met his gaze in the mirror, and she knew from the blaze of heat in his eyes that something she'd said had managed to put a crack in his control. If he were ever going to open up and talk to her, it was now or never.

"Okay," she said as he turned to face her. "Okay. You said it's complicated. More complicated than just sex. Tell me what you mean. Make me understand!"

Chuck took several steps toward her, but then stopped, turning away and running both hands up his face and over his hair to grip the tensed muscles in the back of his neck. He swore, softly but steadily.

"Please?" She reached out to touch his arm.

He pulled away as if she'd burned him. "Maggie, Christ—I can't explain. Not without . . . Not easily."

"Not easily?" The way he'd jerked his arm away from her made her want to cry. "So it won't be easy. Do you think any of this is easy for *me?* Do you think it's going to be easy for me to put on some stupid dress and seduce some stranger who both is and isn't the man I *really* want to be with? I don't want to make love to Charles, I want to make love to *you*." Oh, damn, she'd gone and told him far too much. But now that she'd started, she couldn't seem to stop herself. "Except, he's you. He's part of you, and if I *do* make love to him, I'm making love to you, too, aren't I? And . . . and . . . it's *so* damn *confusing!*"

There were tears in his eyes as he stood there, just looking at her. "Dear God," he whispered, "I've done this all wrong."

SIX

Maggie sat down and closed her eyes, feeling all of the fight draining out of her. He'd done this wrong. He'd made mistakes.

Not half as many as *she'd* made, obviously.

She felt the mattress sink as he slowly sat down on the bed. He didn't move to touch her, he just sat there, next to her.

"Mags, I . . . I've known you for seven years," Chuck said quietly, haltingly. "And I swear, I've wanted you in every way possible for every single second of that time."

She lifted her head, turning to look at him, uncertain of what she'd just heard. "What?"

He gave her one of his crooked half smiles. "Don't make me say it again. Once was hard enough."

Maggie turned toward him. "But . . . "

"I've been fighting like hell to stay away from you these past few days." He reached up with one hand, again as if trying to loosen the muscles in his shoulders and neck. "And yes, you were right. I was trying to set it up so that this time when you met me—Charles—at that party, you'd end up going home with him. See, I thought that might be a way to compress those seven years into just a few short weeks. But we don't have weeks anymore. We don't even have days. Only *hours*. I don't know, maybe it'll still work. See, I thought if I could make Charles feel the same way as I do about you . . ." He took a deep breath as he glanced at her, then shook his head. "I guess I just thought . . . I mean, *I* can't imagine making love to you and then letting you walk away. I guess I thought if I did this right, Charles wouldn't let you walk away, either."

Maggie was watching him silently, her brown eyes subdued. Chuck wanted to reach out and touch her cheek. Her skin looked so smooth and soft. But he knew that touching her was the last thing he should do. "I'm sorry. I said that badly."

"No," she said softly. "You did okay."

"You were right about my having double memories," he told her quietly. "If you and Charles . . ." He couldn't say it, but he knew from her eyes that she knew what he meant. "I guess I figured at least I'd have *that*, because you're right. I'd definitely remember. I haven't quite figured out what it is—maybe some kind of hormonal release that affects certain memory centers of the brain—but even a simple kiss is enough to make a residual memory extremely clear and—" He broke off. He was babbling now, and she was just watching him, her eyes so soft, so warm. He could drown in those eyes.

And still, she didn't speak.

"So now what?" He forced a half smile. "Which one

of us locks ourself in the bathroom until checkout time?"

Maggie touched the side of his face. "How about neither?"

Chuck knew he should stand up and put some distance between them, but he had no strength left. Instead he closed his eyes, allowing himself the forbidden pleasure of her touch. He felt her move closer, felt the softness of her lips where her fingers had been mere seconds before.

He couldn't keep from touching her, too, from gently trailing his fingers down the smoothness of her arms. He felt her shiver and he knew he should stop, but he couldn't. God, he couldn't.

"Chuck?" she breathed.

He opened his eyes. Her mouth was mere inches away from his. At this distance, her eyes were more than brown. He could see dark brown and lighter brown mixed in with flecks of every gorgeous shade in between. She smiled, and even though it was a sad smile, it made her eyes shine. He couldn't keep himself from reaching up and lightly tracing the line of her jaw. She was so beautiful, it hurt.

He had to moisten his lips before he could speak. Even then, his voice came out little more than a whisper. "Yeah, Mags?"

"I want to be with you tonight."

He couldn't answer her. What could he possibly say to that?

"Tomorrow night I'll do what you ask," she told him. "But tonight I want you to make love to me." She kissed him lightly on the mouth, pulling back to look into his eyes and whisper, "Please?"

She kissed him again, and Chuck felt his resistance crumble in a flood of emotion so powerful, he nearly cried out.

And instead of backing away, he kissed her too.

He kissed her deeply, taking possession of her mouth, thrilling at the sound of pleasure she made as he pushed her back onto the bed with him.

Dear, sweet God, he wanted this. He wanted her. He *needed* her. He kissed her even harder and she met him with a fierce passion that took his breath away.

She molded her body around him, tightly gripping the leg he thrust up between hers, pressing herself against him. She was a dizzying mixture of softness and muscles, of sweetness and fire. She was everything he'd ever wanted, everything he couldn't truly have.

Chuck knew he shouldn't run his hands up underneath the edge of her shirt. He knew he shouldn't cup the softness of her breast in the palm of his hand. And he knew the last thing he should do was to caress the tantalizingly erect nub of her nipple and arouse her even further.

But he did and the sounds she made deep in the back of her throat as she kept on kissing him set him on fire.

He knew he should stop. He knew he should back away. Maggie didn't belong to him. She never could.

But when she tugged at his jacket, he helped her pull it off. He unfastened the shoulder holster and that and the gun soon followed the jacket onto the floor. And when she pulled at his T-shirt, that, too, went up and over his head.

And then he kissed her again. The sensation of her hands gliding across the bare skin of his back combined with the soft eagerness of her mouth was dizzying.

Sixty hours. He only had sixty hours left, regardless of his own failure or success. His time was running out, and there was nothing he could do about it.

Except take this moment. He could take these few hours, steal this single taste of paradise.

And he *would* be stealing. Maggie had laid all of her feelings and desires out on the table, leaving herself open and vulnerable.

But he couldn't keep himself from taking advantage. He could no longer resist what he'd wanted for so long.

She'd unbuttoned her shirt and he pushed it off her shoulders, exposing the lace of her bra and the smooth expanse of her stomach. He kissed the tops of her breasts, ran his mouth and hands along all that glorious skin as she reached for the top button on his jeans.

Her fingers brushed against him and the reality of what they were going to do—of what they were doing—was too much. He lifted his head. "Maggie—"

She knew what he was thinking. "This is right," she told him. "We *need* this." She pulled him down on top of her, cradling him between her legs as she kissed him again. "*I* need this. I need you, Chuck."

Her skirt was gone. Somehow she'd managed to free herself from it. She lifted her hips, pressing herself intimately against him, and Chuck knew he was only kidding himself. Even if he had wanted to, there was no way he could stop what they'd started.

And God help him, he didn't want to.

He kissed her, filled with that odd mixture of euphoria and despair as she reached for him again, unfastening his zipper. And then, God, she was touching him.

He pulled back, swiftly kicking his legs free from his jeans and his shorts, even as she unfastened her bra and skimmed her own panties down her legs.

He wanted to stop time, to freeze this moment, to step back and just look at her, Maggie Winthrop, lying naked on his bed, waiting for him, *wanting* him. It was his richest, dearest fantasy come true.

But he knew he couldn't hesitate, he couldn't risk taking the time to form any rational thoughts. Because if he were thinking rationally, he would know damn well that the right thing to do was to stop. To keep this beautiful insanity from going any further.

Maggie reached for him even as he lunged for her, and together they fell back on the bed, skin touching skin, soft flesh against taut muscle.

She was so tiny, so perfect. He felt as if he could crush her, as if it wouldn't take much for him to hurt her badly. Yet she pulled him even closer, as if the weight of his body on top of hers didn't alarm her, as if she trusted him completely.

Chuck wanted to touch her everywhere at once and he skimmed the softness of her skin with his hands and mouth, stroking, caressing, reveling in her sweet smoothness. He explored her most intimate place with his fingers; she was slick and hot and so ready for him. She pushed him over onto his back so that she was on top of him, straddling him, the softness of her belly pressing against his arousal. Her dark hair hung like a curtain around them as she leaned forward to cover his mouth with hers in a hot, sweet kiss. Then she shifted, leaving a trail of kisses along his neck, down his chest. The sensation was so exquisite, he heard himself groan aloud.

He grabbed her then, pushing her back against the bed. Her hair was spread out around her, dark against the white linen.

She smiled up at him with such delight dancing in her eyes.

He couldn't smile back at her, couldn't speak. He could only kiss her, only pray that the waves of emotion that were flooding him would subside before he broke down and wept like a child.

His heart clenched. God help him, God help him, he shouldn't be doing this. He had no right. . . .

"Do you have protection?" she whispered. "A condom?"

Chuck shook his head no. No, this had been the last thing he'd imagined actually happening.

Now they were going to have to stop. Now he would have no choice. He should have felt relief, but the rush of disappointment was so sharp, he had to close his eyes.

"I've got one in my purse," she told him, pushing herself up and off the bed, moving swiftly across the room.

She was back almost instantly, tearing open the foil-wrapped package and handing him its contents.

But it was too late. Sanity had returned. "Mags, we shouldn't do this." God, if only his body would listen to his own words of reason. He knew what he was saying would be far more believable without the extremely obvious proof of his desire for her.

He saw the flare of impatience in her eyes. Impatience, anger, and hurt. "Why not? Where does it say that you shouldn't get what you want? Who the hell are you to say what's wrong and what's right?

"*This* is right," she said, pushing him back against the pillows, straddling him once more, leaning forward to kiss him on the mouth. It was a hard kiss, a punishing kiss, but her lips softened almost instantly, and the rush of need that filled him was dizzying. It didn't seem possible, but he grew even harder with her stomach pressed against him.

"And *this* is right!" She shifted her hips, coming down on top of him, and with one smooth, incredible thrust, he was inside of her.

But the rolled condom was still in his hand.

"Maggie—God!"

Her head was thrown back as she sat above him, moving on top of him, setting a rhythm that echoed the sudden leap of his pulse, and he felt himself slipping toward the edge of a cliff, toward the unstoppable free fall of his own release. The sight of her, her breasts taut with need, her nipples tight peaks of desire, only fueled his desire, and he felt himself sliding faster and faster toward the point of no return.

Nothing, *nothing* had ever felt so good. . . .

He was bigger than she was, stronger, yet he was powerless to stop her, enslaved by his own needs. He wanted her, he needed her.

He loved her.

And he loved her enough to lift her up and off of him.

They couldn't do this. This *wasn't* right.

Maggie protested, and even fought him at first. "No! Chuck—"

He held up the condom he'd damn near crushed in his hand. "These things don't work too well unless you actually put them on."

She watched as he swiftly did just that, her smile tentative. She'd actually thought he'd intended to stop them, to keep them from going any further.

In one swift move, he flipped her onto her back. She reached for him, opening her legs to him, ready to give herself to him so completely. He gazed into her eyes as he entered her slowly, slowly but so deeply she caught her breath at the sensation. Her lips were parted, her eyes dreamy, her lids half-closed as he held himself still inside of her.

And then she smiled, and Chuck knew that his entire life had been building to this one exquisite moment in time.

"This is right," he whispered. "*This* is right."

Her beautiful eyes filled with tears. "Yes," she whispered back. "I think so too."

He kissed her then. Her lips were so soft, so sweet. She lifted her hips, pressing him even farther inside of her, and they both cried out, their voices intermingling in the stillness of the dimly lit room.

He wanted to make love to her slowly, to make this moment last forever. But she urged him on, faster, harder, deeper. He drove himself inside of her, filling her again and again, as the world blurred around him, until there was only now, and only Maggie.

Only Maggie.

She cried out and he felt the beginning of her release. It was completely consuming, wildly overpowering. She clung to him, writhing beneath him, her fingernails sharp against his back.

Her release pushed him over the edge and he exploded in an eruption of pleasure that cannonballed through him. It was a pleasure so sharp and sweet, it seemed to burn him, incinerating him instantly. All coherent thought vanished, and there were only feelings, only warmth.

A sense of peace.

A sweet, perfect sensation of timeless floating.

The scent of Maggie's sweet perfume.

"I think I love you," Maggie whispered, her mouth brushing lightly against his face.

And just like that, he was back. His eyes opened, and reality clicked back in to focus. His scientist's brain was back on-line, and he felt a sinking sense of dread at her words.

She thought she *loved* him.

He rolled off of her, suddenly aware that he was crushing her. He felt her watching him, felt her light brown eyes studying his face, and he forced a smile. She didn't move closer, didn't try to nestle against him or snuggle with him.

He closed his eyes.

God, what he would have given to hear her say those words anytime over the past few years.

But now . . . She *couldn't* love him. She had to love *Charles*.

But he *was* Charles, he reasoned. Maybe this wasn't such a terrible thing. If Maggie could love him, as scarred and jaded as he was, then surely she could love Charles. It only made sense.

Except for the fact that love wasn't rational—love didn't make sense.

Still, perhaps this intimacy they'd just shared would work in his favor. Maybe this physical connection would help to bind Maggie to him—whether he was Chuck *or* Charles.

"Are you asleep?" she whispered.

Chuck opened his eyes to find her still watching him. "No."

"Are you okay?" There was concern in her eyes. Concern and uncertainty.

"Yeah." He reached for her, pulling her against him, molding her back against his front and covering them both with the sheet. Her head was nestled underneath his chin, and he held her close, his arm around her, one hand resting lightly on her breast.

He held her possessively, even though he knew she wasn't his to keep.

This *wasn't* right, what he'd done, what he was doing with her here, tonight. He'd tried to convince himself otherwise in the heat of passion, but now he was face-to-face with the truth. Making love to her and holding her this way as she slept was wrong. But tonight was the only time with Maggie that he had—it was the only time he'd ever have.

And he was taking that time, even though he knew doing so was selfish and cruel.

He knew damn well he couldn't give her what she wanted. He couldn't bring himself to tell her his secrets. He wasn't any good at opening up, at expressing himself.

God, he hadn't even been able to tell her that he loved her.

But that was the least of it.

Sixty hours. Fewer now. If he failed, in less than sixty hours he would be dead.

And if he succeeded . . . If his plan worked, if Maggie could convince Charles to switch his career to medicine, then time travel would never be invented. Wizard-9 would be thwarted, the White House wouldn't be blown up, the president wouldn't die.

And Chuck's current life and the path he'd taken to get here would be instantly erased. His life as he knew it would simply cease to exist.

And Chuck himself would vanish.

SEVEN

Late in the afternoon, Maggie awoke to find Chuck staring at the ceiling.

She lay there for a moment, studying his profile. His mouth was set in its usual grim line, and the muscles in the side of his jaw were jumping. No wonder he frequently gripped and rubbed his forehead and neck—his constantly clenched teeth probably gave him one incredible headache.

Maggie wished she had the power to read minds, to know what he was thinking.

She didn't try to fool herself into imagining that he would ever volunteer that information.

Her stomach rumbled hungrily and he turned his head. "You're awake."

She nodded, wondering when he looked into her eyes if he saw a still-smoldering echo of the love they'd shared in the early-morning light.

Maggie had never experienced anything like that before in her entire life.

It had been wild and raw—by far the best sex she'd ever had. Ever.

But it had been so much more than that too.

She had never felt so connected, so in tune with another human being.

She had never felt so complete.

Except after they'd made love, after they'd exhausted their desire, after he'd pulled her into his arms and held her, he hadn't said a single word.

Maybe it didn't matter. Maybe she didn't need him to talk to her. Maybe his nonverbal skills would make up for his deficiencies in the more traditional types of communication.

She leaned toward him to kiss him, hoping to engage in more of that nonverbal communication.

But Chuck met her lips only briefly before he pulled away. He swung his legs over the side of the bed, sitting for a moment with his back to her. "It's nearly four-thirty. We need to start getting ready."

She sat up, touching his back. "Ready for what? I'm in no hurry to go anywhere." She pressed herself against him as she kissed his shoulder, encircling him with her arms, her hand encountering the muscles of his taut stomach, then sliding even lower. "Are you sure I can't talk you into—"

Chuck caught her hand. "Maggie, we need to go." He stood up, grabbing his jeans from the floor and pulling them on in one swift motion. "If you want to take a shower, you should do it now."

He wanted her, Maggie knew he did. He was far more than half-aroused. It was something of a challenge for him to zip his jeans.

"I want to take a shower—but I want you to take it with me," she said boldly. She stood up, too, making no move to cover herself.

For some reason, he was back to trying to resist her. She didn't know why, but if she had her way, that resistance was going to crumble, and soon.

But when he turned to look at her, the heat and desire that flared in his eyes was tempered with a profound sadness.

"I can't think of anything I'd rather do more," he told her quietly. "But we're running out of time. I need you to intercept Charles before he leaves for the Data Tech party."

He needed her to . . .

"Please, Mags," he continued. "Take a shower, and get dressed."

He turned away, taking the slinky dress from its hanger. As Maggie watched, he disappeared into the bathroom, and she heard him hang it on the back of the door. He came back out, stepping aside for her.

But she didn't move. *Get dressed.* He didn't seriously expect her to put on that dress and . . .

But he did. Maggie saw that fact in his face, in his eyes. He still expected her to use that sexy dress to try to seduce Charles.

No, she couldn't believe that. Not after the way he'd made love to her. She *wouldn't* believe it. He must have something else in mind.

"You said I wouldn't be able to go to the party—that the Wizard-9 agents would be waiting for me!" Her words came out in barely a whisper.

"You aren't going to the party," he told her. "*I* am."

He took one of the bath towels and shook it open. He handed it to her as if hoping she'd use it to wrap around herself. But Maggie still didn't move. She couldn't move.

"But they'll kill you."

"No, they won't. They need Charles alive, remember? To develop the Wells Project. When I go to the party, they'll think I'm Charles."

"I don't understand."

"Ken Goodwin's men are probably watching Charles's condo, because they know that sooner or later I'm going to try to contact him," Chuck explained. "They've probably been following him wherever he goes, only this time they're not going to follow him, they're going to follow *me*. I'm going to get my hair cut and pick up a tux and—"

"You're going to sneak in the back door of the condo and come out the front, pretending to be Charles," Maggie realized.

"That's the general idea," Chuck agreed. "But Wizard-9 is surely watching both the front door *and* the back. There's no way I could get into the condo without being seen."

He took the towel from her hands and gently wrapped it around her. "I was trying to figure out how to make this work when I remembered I left for the party about ninety minutes early. I went into Data Tech to get some work done up in the lab before I had to make an appearance downstairs. But I'd been up late the night before, and before I got into my car, I stopped at the Circle K on the corner to get a cup of coffee to go."

"So Charles will come into the convenience store. . . ."

"And *I'll* come out. I'll take his car and go to Data Tech. The Wizard-9 agents will follow me."

"But if you're both in the Circle K, Charles will see you."

"No, he won't. He'll only see *you*."

This wouldn't work. There had to be a reason why this wouldn't work. Maggie grasped at anything. "How will you get Charles's car keys? If you don't want him to see you—"

Chuck's mouth twisted into a half smile. "You know I don't need keys to start a car."

Maggie drew in a deep sob of air. "So there I am, with Charles in the Circle K. What is it exactly that you expect me to do?" She knew. She just wanted to hear him say it.

His gaze was steady. "You can't go with him back to his place—Wizard-9 probably has the condo bugged. We'll get a suite at the Century Hotel. It's right around the corner. You can take him there."

"You want me to take him to a hotel room."

"Yes."

She hugged the towel tightly. "I can't believe you intend for me to go through with this!" Yes, she'd told him that all she'd wanted was one night, but she couldn't believe after the intensity of what they'd shared . . .

Chuck stood there, dressed only in jeans. Her scent still clung to his skin, his hair was still disheveled from her fingers, and his body was still responding to her nearness.

He was her lover. He was the man she had let steal her heart. But while her eyes may have been filled with tears, his were dry, his face set in an expression of determination.

"We have no choice," he said quietly.

"I'm not going to do it." Her lip was trembling, so she lifted her chin defiantly, hoping the one would cancel out the other and she would look as determined as he did.

He took a step toward her. "Maggie, he's *me*. It's not as if I'm asking you to be with some other man."

"He's *not* you. He's only a part of you. He doesn't even know me!"

He drew his hand through his hair in a gesture of pure frustration. "He *is* me. The same way you're still the same Maggie I've cared so much about for the past seven years."

That stopped her. Was she? Was she truly the same? Chuck had mentioned that the Maggie he had known had changed—that time and a lousy relationship had made her quieter, less sarcastic, perhaps more compassionate and understanding. When Chuck looked at her, did he see a mere shadow of the woman she was to become? Did he miss the maturity and growth that seven extra years of life had surely brought?

Was she nothing more than a poor substitute for the Maggie he truly cared about?

She sank down onto the bed. "Chuck, please. I don't want to be with Charles. I want to be with *you*. Why can't we simply let events play themselves out?"

Chuck didn't reach for her, didn't try to comfort her. Instead he slowly sat on the other bed. "We can't."

Maggie wiped at her face, trying to push away the

flood of emotion that threatened to overwhelm her. "Why not?"

He gazed at her. "Because in approximately fifty-one hours, Wizard-9 will be able to reactivate the Runabout. They'll make another jump—to just a few days into the past this time. And this time they'll get here before me. They'll be waiting to kill me. And then you won't find a naked man in your backyard. You'll find a naked *dead* man."

"Oh, my God! Only *fifty-one* hours . . . ?" Maggie fought a wave of panic.

"The clock's ticking, Maggie. We've got to get moving."

"But . . ." She stared at him, her mind whirling. "Maybe we're going about this all wrong. Maybe instead of trying to keep Charles from developing the Wells Project, we should be trying to find where Wizard-9 has the Runabout. If we could destroy it—"

"That wouldn't be enough. If I'm allowed to continue with my work—" Chuck broke off, shaking his head.

She waited for him to explain, but he didn't say anything more.

She moved toward him then, taking his hands and kneeling on the floor at his feet, prepared to beg if she had to.

"Please. *Why* wouldn't it work? Tell me what you're thinking! Talk to me, Chuck! Tell me what you're feeling! I want to know."

His eyes were a blaze of intensity. "I can't. There are things you shouldn't know about the future."

"I don't give a *damn* about the future. It's all going to

be different now anyway," she said, gesturing toward the bed where they'd shared such incredible love just a few short hours before. "I don't know about you, but *I'm* never going to be the same!"

The sadness in his eyes only deepened, and his words seemed to catch in his throat. If Maggie hadn't known better, she would have thought he was going to cry. "It's not going to be different enough."

Her towel fell off her as she moved up and onto his lap. She held on to him, needing to be closer to him, her arms locked around his neck. "I don't care!"

"Maybe you should." His voice was ragged as he clung to her, holding her as tightly as she held him. "Maggie, you should. God knows *I* care!"

He kissed her fiercely, taking her mouth, stealing her breath, touching her very soul. There were tears on his face. Chuck Della Croce was actually crying.

He seemed to draw strength from her as his hands skimmed the warmth of her body, as he cradled her close to his heart. He kissed her again, softly now, sweetly.

"The day I left my time," he said, his voice a hoarse whisper in the quiet of the room, "only an hour before I appeared in your yard . . . Maggie, I held you while you died."

Maggie couldn't say a word. She had died. She *would* die. Seven years in the future, she was going to die.

"I went to Data Tech," he continued. "You were there. Ken Goodwin didn't know it, but one of the lab cameras was on and you saw the Wizard-9 agents kill Boyd Rogers, my security chief, on the monitor in another lab. You knew I was next, and you tried to warn me.

"We tried to get away, but they started shooting. You stepped in front of me, Maggie, and you took a bullet meant for me." His voice shook. "I locked us both in one of the computer labs, and I held you while you died. Your heart stopped beating, and your eyes glazed over and you were gone. You were *gone*!" He took a deep breath, and when he spoke again, his voice rang with a hard certainty. "I will not let that happen again."

"We can run away," she whispered. "We can destroy the Runabout and then we can hide. You're good at hiding—no one will ever find us."

"We'd have to kill the Wizard-9 agents as well as destroy the Runabout," Chuck said quietly. "If we didn't, they'd simply wait seven years, and then warn themselves about me. They'd let their own selves know about the prototype in my basement, about their failed attempt to kill me. They'd get me before I even left my house that morning." He shook his head. "As long as Charles is out there, they can get to me. And once I'm gone, they'll kill you, too, just to be safe."

Maggie was silent.

"I've got to stop this before it starts." He kissed her gently. "I've opened a terrible Pandora's box," he told her. "Please, Mags, you've got to help me nail it shut."

EIGHT

Checking to make sure his car keys were in his pants pocket, Dr. Charles Della Croce stepped out of the front door of his townhouse condominium, locking it behind him.

The Thanksgiving party at Data Tech didn't start until seven. He was more than an hour and a half early. He was planning to go over now, spend some time in the lab, put in an appearance at the cocktail hour, then leave before the tedium of the actual dinner began.

Unless Maggie Winthrop showed up.

If she showed, without a date, he'd stay for dinner.

He hadn't been able to stop thinking about her since she'd appeared at his table in Papa John's Eatery. He'd done a little investigation and found out that she was, indeed, a freelance writer, hired by the corporation for several short-term projects. He'd dug a little further and found an address for her, and a phone number.

He'd even found out that she'd been issued an invitation to tonight's shindig. But whether or not she was going to attend was still a mystery.

He'd gone as far as calling her to find out if perhaps she'd want to go with him. But he'd only reached her answering machine, and she'd never called him back.

Maybe she was out of town.

Or maybe she wasn't as interested as she'd led him to believe at Papa John's.

Maybe that kiss they'd shared hadn't made her head spin the way his had. He hadn't been able to stop thinking about that kiss.

His car was parked on the street, and as he started toward it a wave of fatigue hit him. He turned, heading for the Circle K on the corner and the self-serve coffee inside.

He'd been up well until dawn the night before, working on his time-travel theories. He was close. He was *so* damned close, but it was still out of his grasp. He'd stayed awake until five-thirty, working the equations, again and again.

He'd slept only two hours before he had to get up and go in to work. He'd told no one at Data Tech about his work with time travel. His theories weren't ready yet for public scrutiny. But maybe soon . . .

He went toward the back of the convenience store, where the brewed pots of coffee simmered on burners. He poured himself a large cup and then turned, searching for the correct-size lid.

"Hello, Charles."

Charles nearly spilled the entire cup of coffee down the front of his tuxedo.

It was Maggie Winthrop. But instead of looking the

way he remembered her, like a sparklingly pretty girl-next-door, the woman who stood before him was pure sensual elegance.

"Remember me? I'm Maggie—"

"Winthrop," he finished for her, setting his cup back on the counter and quickly taking the hand she extended. "Of course I remember you."

Her hair was up off her shoulders—delicately smooth shoulders exposed by the strapless neckline of her dress. And what a dress! It was the richest shade of brown and made of silky material that clung to her breasts. It swept down all the way to the floor, emphasizing her slender waist and the soft curve of her hips.

"I left a message on your home answering machine," he told her with a smile, fighting to keep his gaze properly above her neck. God, she was a knockout! She was wearing makeup—more, at least, than she had on the other time they'd met. It accentuated her soft lips and her gorgeous eyes and the delicate bone structure of her face.

"You did?" Her eyes lit up with genuine happiness.

Charles realized he was still holding her hand. She hadn't tugged it free from his grasp. He held on even tighter, lacing their fingers together, feeling a surge of pleasure. God knows their attraction was mutual. The connection that flowed between them was hot enough to make his coffee seem tepid. But in addition to that attraction, she honestly seemed to like him. As much as he liked her. And he did, he realized. He liked the sparkle in her smile and the amusement that danced in her eyes.

But tonight there was something else in her eyes as well. He could see a quiet sadness that seemed to linger.

"Yeah," he said. "I guess you didn't get my message."

"No, I haven't . . . been home for a while." As he watched she surreptitiously checked her watch. It was a sign that he was either boring her, or she needed to be somewhere. He couldn't believe the first.

"I called to see if you were going to the Data Tech party." He released her hand. "But obviously, you're heading someplace else tonight."

"No, I was planning to go to Data Tech, but not till a little later." She leaned back against the coffee counter, as if she intended to stay for a while. So much for his second theory. "So, what are you doing here? Do you live nearby?"

"Just down the street," he told her. "Are you meeting someone at the party?"

"Actually, I'm supposed to meet *you* there."

Now, what the hell did she mean by that?

"I mean, I was hoping to see you there," she added. She held his gaze, smiling slightly, and he felt his pulse accelerate. Had she come to this particular Circle K hoping to bump into him? He knew her address, and while it wasn't far, this convenience store was anything *but* convenient to her. In fact, it was well out of her way.

"Do you have plans for dinner?" He picked up his coffee and started toward the front of the store, hoping he sounded casual.

"Charles, would you mind pouring me a cup of coffee too?"

He looked at her, startled. For just a moment her voice had sounded slightly strained. But her smile was wide and relaxed. "The decaf's up a little too high," she explained. She leaned forward, closer to him, and lowered her voice. "And I have limited movement in this dress."

The movement she had just made gave him a breathtaking view of the tantalizing fullness of the tops of her breasts. Charles forced his gaze toward the coffeepots. Decaf. She wanted decaf. "Of course," he said, quickly pouring a cup. He put a lid on it as he cleared his throat. "About dinner . . ."

She looked at her watch again. "I've already ordered room service for tonight. I'd love for you to join me."

He picked up both coffees. He wanted to get out of here. He wanted to see Maggie Winthrop in the warm pink light of the lingering sunset. He wanted to offer her his arm and escort her to some four-star restaurant and . . . "Did you say *room* service?"

Charles turned back to her. She took both cups of coffee from him, setting them back on the counter. God, he didn't even think to ask if she wanted cream and sugar.

But cream and sugar wasn't exactly what she wanted. It wasn't even close. She stepped nearer to him, close enough for an embrace, close enough for a kiss, and rested one hand on the front of his jacket, just over his heart. Her other hand went up to the nape of his neck. She gently pulled his head down while rising on tiptoes to meet him and . . .

Her kiss was sheer perfection. Her lips were so soft, her mouth so sweet. He hesitated in surprise for only the briefest of moments before he opened his mouth to her, deepening the kiss. He put his arms around her, pulling her even closer. His hands encountered the cool smoothness of her dress and the perfect softness of her body underneath.

His arousal was instant. He kissed her again, harder this time, pressing her back against the counter. There was no way she could have missed his physical response to her, yet she didn't push him away. On the contrary, she held him even closer, kissing him just as passionately, just as hungrily.

Dear God, he'd died and gone to heaven.

Except when he pulled back to look at her, he couldn't help but see that her eyes were filled with unshed tears. She turned her head, trying her best to blink them away without him noticing.

So he pretended not to notice. "Don't tell me," he said, trying to keep his voice sounding light. It wasn't hard to do because he was breathless. "Someone's following you again."

Maggie gazed up at him. "Actually, someone's following *you*. Agents from a covert government organization called Wizard-9."

Charles laughed. "Wizard-9, huh? Sounds pretty scary."

"Oh, they're very scary." She glanced at her watch again, then picked up the coffee and started toward the front of the store.

Charles followed, taking out his billfold as she set the paper hot cups on the counter near the cash register.

"Anything else?" the clerk asked. He was about seventeen years old and had straggly facial hair that was supposed to pass for a beard. Charles couldn't remember ever being that young.

"No, that's it, thanks."

"A dollar eighty-nine." The kid glanced up at Charles, and did a double take. "You again? What happened to your last cup? Drop it or something?"

"Excuse me?" Charles asked. Him again? He hadn't been in here in days. And even then, this wasn't the same clerk who had waited on him.

"Yeah," Maggie said. "We had a little accident." She handed the boy two dollars.

"A what?" Charles said. "Wait a minute, I'm paying for this."

"You can pay me back," Maggie told him, taking the change, grabbing the coffee, and heading for the door. "Come on."

When she walked, a long slit up the side of the dress revealed flashes of gracefully shaped legs.

Charles was almost completely distracted. Almost. "But why did you say—"

Maggie turned to face him. "Charles, I've got a suite at the Century Hotel. Will you come and have dinner there with me?"

Charles was confused about quite a number of things, but this was not one of them. "Absolutely."

Charles was silent as they took the elevator up to the seventh floor of the Century Hotel, where her suite was located.

Maggie gazed at the numbers above the door, watching the three light up and then the four. She was well aware that Charles's eyes were on her. She was also well aware that he entertained high hopes of having more than dinner here in her room.

Maggie knew what Chuck wanted her to do. He wanted her to have dinner with Charles. He wanted her to be bright and funny. He wanted her to charm him, to be some kind of super, extra-strength, high-dosage Maggie. He wanted her to try to condense seven years of friendship into one short evening.

And he wanted her to cement the whole thing by spending the night with Charles.

But what was she supposed to do after this whole awful mess was over? What was she supposed to do after she succeeded in convincing Charles to change his entire life, his entire career—assuming one glorious night of sex could actually do that. Was she supposed to spend the rest of her life with him?

She glanced out of the corner of her eye at the man standing next to her. He was a stranger—except he wasn't. Not really. He looked like Chuck. He kissed like Chuck. He even smelled like Chuck—a faint but tangy whiff of some kind of aftershave mixed with fresh-smelling soap, commingling with his own very male, slightly musky, extremely delicious scent.

But what else was Charles missing besides the scar on his left cheekbone?

Chuck had desired her—maybe even loved her, although he hadn't admitted as much—for seven years. Charles had met her two days ago.

She'd fallen in love with Chuck. But every experience Charles had lived, Chuck had too. Was it possible, then, to love Chuck without loving Charles as well?

Maggie shook her head. This was much too complicated.

And then there was Chuck. Did he love her? She'd

thought perhaps he did. Last night he'd made love to her so passionately, so emotionally. But maybe he had been simply sating his desire by having sex with someone who looked like the woman he truly cared about—a woman who had died in his arms seven years in the future.

If so, what an incredibly complicated love triangle *that* would be. And if Maggie did what Chuck wanted, she would be involved with Charles, too, making their relationships even more tangled. That couldn't possibly be the solution to *anything*.

Maggie didn't know *what* the solution was, but the first step seemed kind of obvious.

She had to tell Charles the truth.

And as the elevator doors opened onto the seventh floor and they headed down the long, elegantly carpeted corridor to the fancy suite that Chuck had used money from Charles's own bank account to pay for, Charles gave Maggie the perfect opportunity to start telling him the truth.

"So," he said. "What's with the suite at the Century Hotel? Are freelance writers making higher salaries these days than I thought?"

Chuck had prepped Maggie. He'd wanted her to tell Charles that she was staying here because she was having the interior of her house painted and the fumes were too strong.

Instead, as she fitted the key into the lock, she turned to look up at Charles. He was smiling—not that tight, grim little half smile that Chuck so grudgingly gave away. Instead, his face was relaxed, his smile wide. It made him breathtakingly handsome. It lit his eyes, defusing some of the hot attraction that still burned there.

But only some of it.

"Actually, I'm staying here because those men—remember, the ones from Wizard-9 who were following you—they're waiting for me at my home, because they want to kill me." Maggie laughed, and it sounded forced and fake. But now she was babbling and she couldn't stop. "It sounds like one of those brainteasers, the one that goes: There's a man and he wants to go home, but he can't because there are two masked men waiting there for him. You know, it sounds really scary, but it turns out the man is a baseball player on third base, home is home plate, and the two masked men are the catcher and the ump."

Maggie pushed the door open and stepped into the room, praying that after that little outburst Charles wouldn't simply turn tail and run. "Except my own personal brainteaser isn't about baseball. Mine *is* very scary."

She turned and looked back at Charles, who was still standing silently in the hallway. "Are you coming in?"

He hesitated. "Are you . . ."

"Crazy?" she finished for him. "No. I'm sorry, I'm a little on edge. Please. Come in, Charles."

"I wasn't asking if you were crazy." Charles stepped into the room. "I was asking . . . Maggie, are you in some kind of trouble?"

He followed her into the spacious living area of the suite, barely even glancing at the luxurious furnishings, at the gorgeous rose-patterned drapes and matching upholstery. His concern tinged his voice. "Because I have a friend who specializes in getting people out of trouble. I could give him a call and—"

"Boyd Rogers is on leave," Maggie told him, turning to face him.

Chuck had told her about Boyd today as they'd stopped to get his hair cut. Back at that roadhouse, when they'd bought that little illegal gun he wore under his jacket, he'd called Boyd and warned him to make himself invisible. Chuck was afraid Wizard-9 would try to even up their odds by taking Boyd out now, before he became a major player. His old friend had trusted him enough to agree to take a weeklong leave at an unreported destination without a lengthy explanation.

Now Charles *was* staring at her as if she were crazy. Or a mind reader. "How do you know . . ."

Maggie sat down on the rose-patterned sofa. "Charles, I need to talk to you about your work with time travel."

The change that came over him was extreme. One moment he'd been looking at her with concern in his liquid brown eyes. Then it had changed to wariness with her mention of Boyd. Now . . . If a look could cause frostbite, Maggie would definitely require hospitalization.

Still, along with the chill, she could also see curiosity in his eyes. She was counting on that scientist's need to know to keep him from simply walking away.

"What are you talking about? Currently at Data Tech I'm working on—"

"It's not something you're doing at Data Tech. Not yet. Right now you're working on your own."

He took several steps toward the door, but then spun

around and took several steps back. "I haven't told anyone about my theories. How could you possibly know?"

Maggie smiled. "You're probably not going to believe this—but, then again, if *any*one's going to believe it, it's going to have to be you—"

The chill in the room dropped another thirty degrees as his eyes narrowed. "Are you the one who broke into my house a few days ago?"

She shook her head. "No." She crossed her legs, and the slit in the slim skirt of her dress flipped open. His gaze flashed in that direction. Chuck had certainly been right about the physical-attraction thing. It was strong enough to distract Charles even now, when he should have been at his least distractible. "No, I'm not."

"Then who? Someone has. Is it this Wizard-9 you keep talking about . . . ?"

"No. The agents from Wizard-9 are afraid to get too close to you. It's Chuck they want dead."

"Chuck?"

This was not going to be easy to explain. Maggie stood up. "Do you like this dress?"

With a sudden burst of exasperation, Charles ran his hands back through his hair. His mouth was held in a grim line, his eyes burned with intensity, and with the exception of that missing scar on his left cheekbone, he suddenly looked exactly like Chuck. He even sounded like Chuck as he kept his voice carefully tight and controlled. "Will you please just tell me what the hell—"

"I'm *trying*," she said. "Just answer my question."

"Yes," he said. Some of that control slipped. He clearly wasn't as good at holding everything in as Chuck was. "All right? Yes, I like it very, *very* much—"

"You should. You picked it out for me."

"No, I didn't—*God!* Why am I arguing with you about a dress? You're obviously—"

"Sometime within the next seven years, those time-travel theories you're working on will become legitimate enough for Data Tech to sponsor your research," Maggie raised her voice to inform him. It wasn't long before he closed his mouth and listened.

She continued, more quietly. "And sometime within the next seven years the Wells Project will be born and your theories will become reality. Your theories will work, Charles, but some very bad people from an organization called Wizard-9 will want to get their hands on your time-travel device—you call it a Runabout. They'll use it to go back in time and plant a bomb in the White House that will kill the U.S. President, and then they'll try to kill you too. But you'll escape, and you'll use a prototype to come back in time to try to set things right."

Charles slowly sat down. "My God."

"You'll come back from the future, and one of the things you will do is to pick out this dress for me to wear—a dress that's sure to catch your attention." She sat down across from him. "There are two Dr. Charles Della Croces in Phoenix right this very moment. One of you is thirty-five years old, the other is forty-two. Your forty-two-year-old self—he calls himself Chuck—he's at Data Tech right now, pretending to be you.

"He was in the Circle K with me when you arrived. While I kept you busy he bought a cup of coffee and went out. He took your car over to Data Tech, and the agents from Wizard-9 followed him, thinking he was you.

"You see, Wizard-9 wants to make sure Chuck and I do nothing that will prevent you from developing your time-travel theories. They're following you to make sure we don't get close to you."

Charles was silent, just watching her. Then, as if he couldn't hold it in any longer, he leaned forward, spearing her with the intensity of his gaze. "How does it work?" he asked. "Where have I been going wrong in my equations? Is it the—"

"Whoa." Maggie held up her hand. "I don't know anything about the theories."

"God, I can't believe it actually works!"

He stood up in one swift motion, reaching across the coffee table to pull her to her feet. He grabbed her around the waist and whirled her around the room. "It works, God, it really works!"

Maggie laughed at his totally un-Chuck-like outburst. She'd never seen him act like this before. She hadn't known he was capable of such sheer, unadulterated joy.

But as quickly as he'd started to dance, he stopped. He nearly ran to a small writing desk that sat near the entrance to the room. He opened the drawers, rifling through them until he came up with paper and a pen. He quickly brought them back to the sitting area, and leaning against the coffee table, he began to scribble what looked like equations as he mumbled aloud.

Maggie's strengths didn't lie in mathematics, but she knew one thing. He had to have a mind like a computer to be able to think in terms of the kind of equations he'd just scratched onto that piece of paper.

For the first time she fully realized how incredibly intelligent Charles Della Croce was. For so long she'd thought of Chuck as a kind of a cowboy, a gunslinger, a fighter. But in truth, Chuck *was* Charles, and he was also a brilliant scientist.

She wished, though, that he hadn't forgotten how to smile, to laugh, to break into spontaneous dance.

As she'd seen Chuck do nearly a dozen times, Charles seemed to become aware that he was drumming his fingers impatiently on the tabletop. And just as she'd seen Chuck do, he forced himself to stop.

He was so like Chuck, but even so, she could see the differences. Charles didn't have that hard edge, that suspiciousness, that hard-as-steel toughness that made Chuck seem impenetrable. He still had that same piercing intensity, but he also had a charming touch of youth and innocence—that ability to become genuinely excited.

Both men had the habit of keeping themselves slightly distanced from her by both their body language and a certain detachment in their eyes. She'd broken through Chuck's control a few times, but it had required tremendous patience and hard work.

Charles's control seemed far less anchored in place.

As Maggie watched he threw down the pen and raked his fingers through his hair. "What am I doing? All I have to do is talk to . . . my other self. He can tell me where I'm going wrong. Chuck, right?" He paused. "Why does he call himself Chuck?"

"Because I gave him that nickname," Maggie told him.

He looked at her. Really looked at her. Maggie could practically see the wheels turning in his head. "Are we lovers?" he asked quietly. The chill in his eyes was completely gone. He smiled slightly, almost shyly. "Please say yes."

She nodded. "Yes," she said. "Lovers—and friends."

Charles nodded too. "That's a good combination."

Maggie had to look away. "Chuck doesn't seem to think so."

"Of course he does. I should know because he's me, right? I'm him." He smiled again. "It's funny, when we first met, I had this odd sensation, as if I knew you already—and in a sense I did. Only it was in the future that I knew you, not in the past." He stood up again as if he couldn't sit still another moment. "God, I can't believe it's really going to *work!* Do you know how many years I've been working on these theories?"

Maggie shook her head. "No." Chuck hadn't told her. Chuck hadn't told her much of anything about himself.

"For more than twenty-five years," he said. "I started the basis of these theories back when I was seven years old."

"Why?" she asked, leaning forward slightly. "Why is developing time travel so important to you?" Maybe *Charles* would tell her. . . .

But he didn't answer right away. He just looked at her. "It is," he finally said. "It's very important to me. Ever since—" He broke off. "I haven't told you anything about it?"

Maggie shook her head. "Sharing's not exactly one of your strengths."

He changed the subject. "You said I came back in time to 'set things right.'"

She met his gaze. "That's right. Seven years from now your top priority will not be to develop time travel. It'll be to make sure you *don't* develop it. Charles, that's what I'm here to ask you to do. Stop your research. Don't let it go any further."

She'd shocked him. She saw it clearly in his eyes. Chuck never would have let it show. "How can I stop when I'm obviously so close to success?"

"Because if you *don't* stop, hundreds of people will die. Including *you.*"

He silently started to pace.

Maggie turned on the couch to face him. "Chuck seemed to think you would do well to go into medical research and—"

"But it's all going to be different now," Charles interrupted her. "Now that I know what's going to happen, I can make sure this Wizard-9 isn't involved in the project."

"There's no way you can do that. They'll kill you and steal the Runabout if they have to."

"So what am I supposed to do? Burn my papers? Erase my computer files? Promise never even to *think* about time travel ever again?"

"Yes," Maggie said. "Please."

He stopped pacing. That wasn't what he'd expected her to say. He stared down at her. "Are you sure you want me to do that?" he asked. "Just like that, everything will be different. One tiny seemingly inconsequential decision, and my entire life will take an absolutely different path."

"And a lot of people won't die because a bomb *isn't* planted at the White House. And you won't become the target for assassins and terrorists and other crazies who want to get their hands on the Wells Project. And Wizard-9 agents *won't* chase you across the better part of a decade, trying to kill you before you have the chance to change what they've already done."

He stepped toward her, gently touching her cheek with one finger. "And we might never meet. Are you willing to risk that, Maggie?"

"But we *have* met," she countered. "We're here, right now—"

"Are we?" he asked. "I'm here, but are you? Are you from the future? Because if you are, if I make that one little seemingly inconsequential decision, you're going to disappear. You and Chuck will vanish."

Vanish?

"Think about it," he said. "If I don't continue, the Wells Project won't happen. I won't invent the Runabout. . . ."

"I'm not from the future. But . . . Oh, my God," she whispered. "If you don't invent the Runabout, there'll be no way for Chuck to travel back in time and—" She broke off, staring up at Charles. If Charles didn't invent time travel, Chuck wouldn't have come in the first place. None of the events of the past few days would have happened—including Chuck's appearance in her backyard. Charles was right. If he did what she asked and turned his back on his time-travel research, Chuck would simply disappear. "Will I even remember that he was here? Will I remember him at all?"

There was compassion in his eyes. "I don't know."

Maggie closed her eyes, remembering the way Chuck had kissed her in the dressing room of the tuxedo shop. They were about to leave for the convenience store, to intercept Charles, and Chuck had pulled her into his arms and kissed her so sweetly, so tenderly. She realized now that that had been a kiss good-bye. He'd fully intended never to see her again.

She remembered how Chuck had cried back in the motel when he'd told her how she would die, seven years in the future. She remembered the steely determination in his voice as he swore he wouldn't let it happen that way this time around.

She hadn't realized it, but he was prepared to give up everything for her. Even his own existence.

Right now he was at the Data Tech party, all alone, waiting for himself to cease to be. He knew that if Maggie succeeded, he would disappear. With just—what had Charles called it?—one little seemingly inconsequential decision, the past seven years of Chuck's life, everything he'd done and dreamed and hoped and felt, would be gone.

Maggie stood up. Her legs felt weak, and her voice sounded just as wobbly. "I have to find Chuck." She headed for the door. "Come on, Charles, you've got to help me. We've got to go to Data Tech, and you've got to trade places with Chuck again. I have to talk to him. There's got to be another way."

NINE

Chuck worked his way through the crowded Data Tech lobby, heading for the bank of pay phones, careful not to let the Wizard-9 agents get too close.

He'd put some makeup on his scar. From a distance it looked fine. But up close, it wouldn't take long for someone who knew him as well as Ken Goodwin did to figure out that he was the older-model Della Croce.

The way things were going, it was only a matter of time before his real identity was exposed.

He couldn't *believe* the memories that were flooding through him.

Maggie had taken his plan and tossed it right out the window. Instead of trusting that Chuck would know the best way to manipulate his own past self, she had decided to go for the direct approach with Charles. She'd actually gone and told him the truth.

The *truth*.

Chuck cursed himself for a fool. This was his fault. He should have explained to Maggie why telling Charles the truth was a very, very bad idea. He should have told her about that goddamned game of Chinese checkers he didn't play when he was seven. He should have told her that Charles had an extremely powerful and compelling reason to want to continue his time-travel research. Telling him that time travel was possible, and that it was within reach, within less than a decade's worth of work—that wasn't the way to get him to quit.

And now Maggie and Charles were coming here, to Data Tech. He knew even when he dialed the phone that no one would pick up at the suite in the Century Hotel. He knew that if he could remember riding in a taxi alongside of Maggie, then they were already on their way over.

Chuck ran his hand through his hair as he tried to think. Think. He *had* to think. He would continue to be a step behind them if he waited for the memories to kick in. He would remember the door Charles and Maggie came in only *after* they came through it. And when he got there, they'd be gone.

Unless he could remember their conversation. But this time his memories were ghostly and faded, as if everything Maggie and Charles were doing really *did* take place seven years ago. It was hard enough to remember their actions, let alone their words.

No, his best bet would be to second-guess them.

Okay. That shouldn't be too hard. After all, he *was* Charles. What would he do?

He's just been told that his time-travel theories are on the right track. He's jazzed by that, *and* by the fact that he's in the company of an incredibly attractive woman. The potential danger only heightens the excitement he feels. What would he do?

Maggie wouldn't know that Ken Goodwin had augmented his forces, hiring outside help and nearly doubling his number of men. She would have told Charles that there were only four Wizard-9 agents. He'd figure with such limited manpower, Wizard-9 would either watch the back entrances, or keep an eye on the man they thought to be Charles.

And he and Maggie would waltz in through the front door, hoping to be lost in the crowd.

Chuck took the stairs up to the second floor and stood leaning on the railing overlooking the sculpture of a flock of birds in flight. He pretended he was part of a conversation between two vice-presidents and an office manager. He laughed when they laughed, nodded when they nodded, all the while scanning the crowd in the lobby below.

And then he saw them—Maggie in that incredible dress. The sight of her made his heart stop. She had her hand in the crook of Charles's arm as they walked toward the building from the well-lit parking lot. Despite their differences in height, they made a very handsome couple.

Chuck felt a surge of jealousy and anger that he didn't bother to squelch. With a sudden flash of clarity, he could remember what he was thinking, what he was feeling down there as he walked with Maggie on his arm. And he wasn't thinking about Maggie's safety. He wasn't thinking about Maggie hardly at all. He was focusing on his damned theories and equations, on the prospect of meeting his future self and having all of his questions answered. He was an idiot, a fool.

And Maggie . . . Maggie was looking through the glass front of the lobby, searching for him. She found him almost right away, and their gazes locked. Despite the distance and the pane of glass between them, it was as if she had reached out and touched him.

She was angry, she was hurt, she was scared. He could see all that in her eyes. And she loved him. He saw that too.

She wanted to be with him, and God, he wanted the same. But the only way that could ever happen was by talking Charles into giving up his work with time travel. Only then did they even have a chance. He wanted to grab his past self by the neck and shake him until he realized what he had right underneath his nose. Maggie. He had Maggie.

Chuck saw two different cars pull up directly behind Charles and Maggie, and then everything seemed to switch into slow motion.

The doors of both cars opened and several very big men dressed in dark suits burst out. Charles spun around in surprise as they grabbed both him and Maggie and began pulling them toward the open doors of the cars.

As Chuck watched in horror Maggie fought to get away, and one of the dark-suited men grabbed her around the waist. She fought even harder, kicking and scratching and biting. And screaming.

Chuck couldn't hear a thing. The glass windows that separated them kept all outside noise from the lobby.

It was surreal. Inside, the party guests sipped their

drinks, talked, and laughed, while just outside an abduction was taking place.

It was as if he were watching a silent movie. He couldn't hear Maggie, but he could read her lips.

She was shouting his name, over and over again.

As Charles and Maggie were shoved none too gently into two separate cars, Chuck couldn't help himself. *"Maggie!"* He sprang over the side of the railing, dropping heavily to the tiled floor of the lobby below.

Someone screamed, several other people dropped their drinks in alarm, and a murmur of voices rose up.

He scrambled to his feet, rushing out toward the parking lot.

But all he saw were taillights as the cars sped away.

Chuck turned back to the lobby doors, well aware that he was the subject of a great deal of attention. In a flash of realization, he knew that he'd given himself away. Sure enough, he could see at least one of the Wizard-9 agents fighting to get to him through the crowd.

Chuck turned and ran.

"It occurs to me that you might be of more use to us dead than alive."

Maggie lifted her chin, giving the man who sat having a late lunch at the poolside table her best version of the evil eye. "My tax dollars pay your salary, don't they? What a terrible waste."

Ken Goodwin just smiled. He had a bland, almost round, friendly face. His wire-rim glasses made him look doubly harmless. Maggie knew he was anything but.

"Dr. Della Croce is very attached to you," he noted

in his vowel-flattened New England accent. "And you to him."

Maggie gave nearly all of her attention to a rough spot on her thumbnail. "So?"

Goodwin laughed. "Did he tell you that in his time line, you were married to someone else? He must've yearned for you for years—it's very romantic. Still, he managed to hide his feelings quite well. I'd known him for quite some time, and I didn't suspect a thing."

The afternoon sun was warm on the back of her neck. It felt good after being locked in the chill of the house since last night. Maggie looked up. "What's your point?" she said flatly.

"By killing you, we seem to have sent Dr. Della Croce into a state that I call self-righteous rage. It appears most commonly in war zones, when an entire platoon of soldiers is decimated by a single man. That man is usually defending his farm or his family. Or avenging their deaths. He's got the advantage of knowing the territory and he's driven by this inhuman power, this self-righteous rage."

Ken Goodwin motioned to his men, both of whom carried lengths of rope, and they hoisted Maggie to her feet. They were neither rough nor gentle—they were simply intent upon getting the job done. And that job seemed to be to lash her hands behind her back and tie her feet together.

Maggie pulled away. "Get away from me!"

But her hands were already tied, and strain as she might against the rope, she couldn't get free. Together, the two men had no trouble binding her ankles.

They lifted her up, but Ken Goodwin stopped them

with a single gesture. "Not yet," he told them, then turned back to Maggie.

"What we've got to do," he continued, "is push Dr. Della Croce—the one you call Chuck—further over the edge. We've got to make him react rather than act. We've got to lure him here into *our* territory. Then we can take care of him and clean up this nasty little mess he's made."

"Take care of him? You mean, *kill* him."

His smile didn't warm his eyes. "He's already dead. He was listed as one of the missing in the Data Tech lab explosion."

Goodwin looked up toward the house, toward a large picture window on the second floor. "Good, now we can continue," he murmured.

Maggie turned and saw Charles standing in the window, one of the agents holding tightly to his arm. Thank God he was safe. She hadn't seen him since last night, when the Wizard-9 agents had pulled him into one car and her into another. She hadn't even been sure that he was here, at this luxurious ranch well on the outskirts of town.

"I've read Dr. Della Croce's work on double memories," Goodwin told her. "Fascinating concepts. Apparently since Charles here is a younger version of the other Dr. Della Croce, everything he experiences—everything he sees and hears and feels—appear as memories in the older man's mind."

It had worried Maggie that they hadn't blindfolded her as they brought her here, but now she realized that Ken Goodwin *wanted* her and Charles to know where they were—so that Chuck would know too. So that he would come here, to rescue her. So they could catch him and kill him, here on their own territory.

Maggie felt fear slice through her as she gazed up at Charles. She had to talk to him. She had to tell Chuck, through him, not to come.

As she watched through the window Charles turned to the man holding his arm and spoke to him questioningly, gesturing down at her. The man said something back, with a grin.

Goodwin nodded to the men who had tied Maggie up, and they each took hold of one of her arms.

"Hey!" Maggie said as they began dragging her backward. "What are you doing?"

Up at the second-floor picture window, she could see Charles break free from the man who was holding him. He rushed toward the glass as if he were trying to go straight through it. But it stopped him and he pressed his hands against it as he shouted her name, loud enough for her to hear.

And then Maggie felt nothing behind her. Nothing but air as the two men pushed her out and back. With a splash, she went into the swimming pool.

Her hands and feet were tied.

She was in water over her head, and her hands were tied securely behind her back.

Panic engulfed her as completely as the water surrounded her.

She tried to kick her legs, to push herself back to the surface, but the weight of her long dress only dragged her down.

Maggie fought as her lungs burned and her heart

pounded. She fought on, knowing that this was a fight that would be very hard to win.

"Get her out of there! Right now! Goddammit, get her *out* of that pool!"

Charles felt the Wizard-9 agent's nose break as he drove the heel of his hand hard into the man's face. It was enough to make the man loosen his elbow lock around Charle's neck. Another hard jab to the man's throat, and he was free. There were no rules. This was street fighting at its harshest, its dirtiest.

And Charles had the advantage. From the way his opponent was pulling his punches, he suspected it was a priority that he be kept alive—and not just alive, but in good health.

He didn't stop yelling at the top of his lungs, screaming his rage like a madman, as he scrambled away from the Wizard-9 agent. He grabbed a chair and swung it with all of his strength across the room at the door as it opened. Two more Wizard-9 agents ducked to avoid being hit. "You bring her up here to me *right now!*"

The room was trashed. And what furniture hadn't been bumped into or knocked over in his fight with the first bruiser, Charles went for now, throwing end tables and lamps—anything that he could pick up—toward the open door. "Now, goddammit! I want her up here *now!*"

He'd never experienced such a surge of fear as when he'd watched Maggie tossed so casually into the swimming pool, her hands and feet tied. He barely knew her, and most of what he knew about her was based on sheer attraction. Yet the thought of her death made him crazy.

He'd never felt this kind of anger before. Or this kind of helplessness.

The agent he'd been fighting lumbered groggily to his feet inside the room, blood streaming from his nose. He turned toward the door, and Charles turned to look, too, brandishing a floor lamp, ready to use it as a weapon against whomever might be trying to come in.

But it was Maggie. Soaking wet and coughing up water, she was pushed into the room, like some sort of sacrificial virgin sent to appease his monstrous anger. Her hands and her feet were still tied, and she fell heavily onto the floor.

Charles's relief was dizzying. Maggie was alive. She wasn't still lying on the bottom of that swimming pool. He dropped the lamp with a clatter and went to her, pulling her up into his arms.

She was shaking and gasping and getting him nearly as wet as she was, but he didn't give a damn. She was alive!

He looked up toward the still-open door and into the eyes of the man who had introduced himself as Ken Goodwin—the head of Wizard-9.

"We weren't really going to harm her," Goodwin said chidingly, looking around at the mess and shaking his head. "We were just trying to get a little message to your future counterpart."

He was lying. Charles knew it. Goodwin was lying. He'd had every intention of letting Maggie drown at the bottom of that swimming pool. It was only because Charles had gone ballistic that they'd pulled her out. Goodwin had been afraid that Charles was going to injure himself in some way, and rather than risk that, he'd let Maggie live.

Charles looked away from Goodwin, afraid the other man would see his sudden realization in his eyes. He had the power. Goodwin and his men from Wizard-9 may have been the captors, but Charles had the ultimate power.

They needed him, and they needed him alive.

Goodwin held up a thickly bound set of papers. It looked like the reports the R&D staff at Data Tech often put together. "I have all the answers to your questions about time travel right here, Dr. Della Croce."

Maggie struggled to sit up. "No! Don't look at it, Charles—"

Goodwin stepped closer. "Why don't we let Miss Winthrop get dried off while Dr. Della Croce and I talk?"

"You *can't* look at it," Maggie continued, her voice as urgent as her eyes. "Charles, please. It's important that you don't ever allow yourself to know how the Wells Project works."

"But, Maggie—"

"Maggie is obviously not a scientist, Doctor," Ken Goodwin interrupted. "She doesn't understand your need to know. Let my men take care of her while you read this report." He motioned two of the agents forward.

Charles would've sold his soul to see inside the covers of that report. But he wouldn't sell Maggie's. He pushed her behind him. "No. She stays here with me or we don't talk at all."

Goodwin sighed.

"Call your men off," Charles said warningly.

"We can do this the easy way or the hard way," Goodwin told him.

Charles didn't hesitate. "The hard way. She stays with me."

Goodwin motioned to the other agents, and they backed off. "All right," he said. "The hard way it is."

TEN

Maggie's hands and feet were still tied, and even after Charles set her down on the floor, he held on to her to keep her from falling over. The door shut, but only after Ken Goodwin tossed the Wells Project report into the closet after them.

They were locked in an empty walk-in closet. A single bulb burned overhead as a full set of bolts were thrown on the outside of the door.

This was Ken Goodwin's hard way. He was pitting Charles and Maggie against each other by putting them here, in such close quarters, with nothing but a light and the report that Charles so desperately wanted to read.

The report that Maggie so desperately *didn't* want him to read.

In the meantime Goodwin was sitting tight, waiting for Chuck to show up and attempt to rescue them. Waiting for him to come into Wizard-9's territory. Waiting to kill him.

"Are you all right?" Charles asked, his eyes dark with concern.

"Charles, you have to help me get a message to Chuck," Maggie said as he helped her down into a sitting position on the carpeted floor. Her dress and hair were still soaking wet, and she blinked water out of her eyes as she looked up at him. "We have to warn him not to come here."

He looked around the tiny closet. "We have to find a way out of here."

"I was locked in here last night," Maggie told him. "The air-conditioner vent is too small—believe me, I already tried. The only way out is through the door. No, we're in here until they let us out—until you read that report, or until Chuck comes and they kill him. And *that's* why we have to warn him to stay away!"

"Warn him through double memories." Charles bent down and worked to untie the rope that lashed her feet together. His fingers were warm against her chilled skin. He glanced at her. "Can they really be that clear? Clear enough to remember a conversation—a warning?"

"Double memories can be pretty faint. At first it feels like a weird kind of déjà vu. But Chuck said that once you get used to—" Maggie broke off, remembering something else Chuck had said. Something about . . . ? "Charles, kiss me."

He glanced up at her in surprise.

"There was something Chuck told me about double memories and glandular activity. If you kiss me, he'll remember."

Charles hesitated. "Maggie, I don't—"

She pulled her still-bound feet away from him and

struggled to her knees. It wasn't easy with the sodden weight of her dress dragging against her legs and with her hands still tied behind her back.

"This *will* work," she insisted. "Kiss me."

He leaned forward, obviously doing this only to humor her. Softly, gently, almost chastely, he brushed his lips against hers.

"Oh please," Maggie scoffed. "I'm not your grandmother. *Kiss* me, Charles. Come *on!* Make it memorable!"

His eyes flared with heat and he pulled her against him so forcefully that nearly all the air was squeezed from her body. And then he kissed her, sweeping his tongue possessively into her mouth, stealing all that was left of her breath.

It was a kiss of pure fire, pure passion. And Maggie kissed him back just as fiercely, just as hungrily, opening herself to him.

He kissed her harder, deeper, inhaling her, consuming her, and her heart pounded wildly as heat surged through her veins.

It was a kiss that *she* would never forget.

"Don't come here, Chuck," she murmured breathlessly, kissing him again and again, praying that her words would stand out in his memory. She had to believe he'd remember. Chuck had remembered their conversation when she'd met Charles at that lunch place in Scottsdale. He'd remembered telling her about carrot cake. He'd remembered *that* kiss. "It's a trap—Goodwin and his men are ready for you. They're hoping you'll make a mistake, that you'll lose your temper and patience. But there's still time. I'm all right. I'm with

Charles now and we're safe for the moment. Whatever you do, be careful. Think it through."

She kissed Charles again, telling herself it was only to drive home her words. It wasn't because she wanted to lose herself in the strength of his passion, in the heat of his hunger for her.

Charles was breathing hard as he pulled back to gaze down into her eyes. He cupped her face with the palm of one hand and traced her lips with his thumb. "What is it about you?" he breathed. "What is this power you have over me?"

Maggie lost herself in the midnight depths of his eyes. Eyes so like Chuck's. "Maybe it's destiny," she whispered. "Or maybe it's knowing that in the future we'll be lovers."

He lowered his mouth to hers and kissed her again, so softly this time, so sweetly. Maggie felt herself melt.

"For you, we're lovers right now," he told her. "But I've got to wait seven years. Seven *years.*" He gave her a crooked half smile that was so like Chuck's. "Something tells me, as much as I'd like to, it's a little too soon to start the foreplay."

Maggie laughed. When she'd been at the bottom of that swimming pool, she had been so sure she'd never have the chance to laugh ever again.

"Let me get these ropes off of you." He gently pushed her back so that he could untie the rope that bound her feet.

"Charles, thank you."

He glanced up at her as he finally worked the ropes loose. "For letting you communicate with Chuck through me?" He gave her another crooked smile. "It was my pleasure. Literally."

Maggie couldn't keep from wincing as he pulled the rope from her ankles.

Charles looked down and saw that the rough cord had rubbed her skin raw as she'd fought to free herself in the swimming pool. "Oh, God, I'm sorry!" He pulled her feet up and onto his lap. "I wasn't being careful—that must've hurt!"

"I'm okay," she said softly. And she was. She was alive. "You know, I really thought I was going to drown. I thought . . ." She shook her head.

"You thought Ken Goodwin was going to kill you," he continued her thought, "because he figured that Chuck—that *I*—had traveled through time to try to save you once already. If you're dead, that gives Chuck a powerful reason *not* to terminate the Wells Project before it even starts. In fact, Goodwin's probably banking on the fact that if you're dead, Chuck's going to work to keep the Wells project alive so that he can have another chance to go back in time and save you."

Maggie shivered. The closet, like the rest of the house, was cold. It was November in the desert, and although the days were warm, the nights could be quite chilly. And the sun wasn't hot enough during the day to heat this big house. "If Goodwin wants me dead, why didn't he just let me drown?"

"Because I wouldn't allow that. We've got to get you out of that wet dress." Charles gently took her feet from his lap and moved around to begin untying her hands.

Maggie turned to look back at him. "That room they

brought me to. The furniture in the room you were held in was wrecked. What did you do?"

He glanced into her eyes. "I played what turns out to be our trump card."

She could feel her wrists burn as he tugged gently at the rope and she couldn't keep from drawing in a sharp breath.

"Maggie, I'm sorry. Your wrists are pretty scraped up too. I don't think I can get this rope off without hurting you."

"Just do it. I'll be okay."

He did. It took several long, agonizing seconds, but then the rope finally was off of her. Her fingers were numb and her shoulders ached as she pulled her hands in front of her. "What trump card?" she asked Charles, trying to ignore the tears of pain that were stinging her eyes. She pushed her wet hair out of her face and hiked up her soggy dress as she turned to face him.

"Goodwin needs me alive," Charles told her. "That's how we're going to get out of here. I'm going to hold my own self hostage."

Maggie shook her hands, trying to bring life back into her numb fingers. "How? We don't have enough time for a hunger strike. And I doubt threatening to hold your breath until you turn blue is going to work."

Charles gave her a quick smile. "I haven't quite figured out the how part yet, but I'm working on it." He shrugged out of his fight-tattered jacket and began taking off his tuxedo shirt.

Maggie couldn't help but notice when he glanced down at the Wells Project report still lying on the floor. It was only a matter of time before he reached for it. But right now his priorities were with her. "Come on," he said gently. "Get out of that dress before you catch pneumonia. You can put on my shirt and jacket."

Maggie didn't move, and he turned around so that his back was to her. "I won't look," he added.

Maybe he *should* look. Maybe that would keep him from looking at the Wells Project report instead.

Maggie closed her eyes, still feeling the fire of his kisses. "I can't get the zipper. My fingers . . ." It wasn't quite true, but he wouldn't know that.

She heard him turn around, felt him touch her gently as he searched for the tiny zipper pull on the back of her dress. The sound of the zipper going down seemed to echo in the silence.

There was no way he could miss the fact that she wasn't wearing a bra. In fact, he probably already knew that from the way the wet fabric of the dress was glued to her like a second skin. Her breasts were clearly outlined, her nipples taut from the cold. Still, the unavoidable intimacy of her completely bare back—bare from the nape of her neck all the way down to the lace of her panties—exposed by the simple pull of a zipper made it obviously clear.

She could hear him swallow, hear his quiet breathing. She could hear her own heart beating in that fraction of a second between her decision and her ability to act.

And then Maggie acted. She pulled the dress off, stepping out of it as it sank in a heavy wet pile on the floor. She didn't know if Charles had turned around to give her privacy, but she had to guess from the way he wrapped his shirt around her that he hadn't.

She turned to face him, pulling the shirt off her shoulders.

He was wearing only his tuxedo pants, and he looked like some kind of exotic male stripper. And she—she was wearing only slightly more than he had been wearing that day, seven years in his future, when she'd first set eyes on him.

Chuck had wanted her to seduce Charles. He seemed to think that Maggie would have no trouble at all, that Charles would be unable to resist her. And from the sudden volcanic flare of heat in Charles's eyes at the sight of her wearing only the white lace of her panties, it seemed as if he was right.

But Charles was not just a man. He was a brilliant man. And the crooked smile he gave her was rueful. "Boy, you *really* don't want me to look at that report, do you?"

Maggie felt herself blush as he reached for the shirt in her hands and held it open for her. Closing her eyes in embarrassment, she slipped her arms into the sleeves. He turned her to face him, and began buttoning the front, as if she were a child.

"Now would probably be a good time for you to tell me exactly why you don't want me to read that report," he continued.

"I'm not sure I can speak and die of embarrassment at the same time," she told him.

He caught her chin with his hand, tipping her head up, and she opened her eyes to find herself looking directly into his eyes.

"I think I'm probably going to spend the rest of my life regretting that I didn't seize the moment and take advantage of you." He smiled crookedly. "God, I don't just think it—I *know* it."

For one brief moment Maggie was certain that he was going to lean forward and kiss her again. But instead of covering her mouth with his, he released her, stepped back, and put some distance between them.

"But you belong to someone else," he continued quietly. "Someone that I'm not—not yet, anyway. And as much as I'd like to let you . . . distract me, it wouldn't be right."

Maggie turned away, picking up the sodden mass of her dress, trying to hide the emotion that surged through her at his soft words. She hung her dress over one of the bars that stretched lengthwise across the small space. "Funny, I was just thinking how like him you are." She turned to face him. "You have to promise me that if . . . something *does* happen to me—"

"I'm not going to let anything happen to you—"

She took a step toward him. "Charles, they have guns and we don't. Think about it. If Chuck doesn't storm the gates, trying to get us out, and if you don't read the Wells Project report, I'm willing to bet that by the time the sun sets, Ken Goodwin will stop trying to persuade you to see things his way—he'll start using force. And the first thing he'll do is take *me* out of the picture—permanently. And Chuck will want to find a way to go back in time again, to save me. Again."

Charles reached for the report, still lying on the floor. "So maybe I should do what Ken Goodwin wants."

Maggie moved faster, putting her foot on it before he could pick it up. "I'm afraid if you read this, there'll be no turning back. I'm afraid once you understand the theories and the equations you used to make the Runabout work, you won't be able to change your entire destiny with just one simple decision. I'm afraid that what you learn will take you past the point of no return."

Charles sat down on the floor, leaning back against the wall and tiredly taking off his black dress shoes. "Maggie, you have no idea how badly I want to look at that report."

She sat down next to him. "Really? Even knowing that in seven years you'll be willing to trade your entire life for a chance to walk away from the information that's in there?"

He was silent.

"If Chuck were here right now," she told him, "he'd be urging you to take all of your theories on time travel and just let them go. He'd tell you that you have the power to end this once and for all. Right here. Right now. All you need to do is make that decision. No, you won't work on time travel anymore. Yes, you'll go back to school, finish up your medical degree, and start working full-time on finding a cure for AIDS. Or cancer. Or *some*thing. Something good. Something that can't be used as a weapon by unscrupulous people."

"If I do that," Charles said quietly, "if I decide right now to do that, you won't ever see Chuck again."

Maggie felt her eyes fill with tears. "I know."

"What if there's some way we can make this work?" Charles turned to face her, taking her hand and lacing their fingers together. "What if there's something Chuck's overlooked, something he hasn't come up with, some way we can stop Wizard-9 and *still* develop my time-travel theories?" he asked. "Maggie, I want to talk to him. I want to figure out a way to get us safely out of here so we can meet him somewhere and try to figure this out."

Maggie looked into the dark brown intensity of his eyes. Chuck's eyes. "Why is this so important to you?" she whispered. "Why do you want to develop time travel so badly? What happened that you want so desperately to go back and do over?"

As she watched, she saw him take an emotional step back, away from her. His face was instantly more reserved, his eyes almost shuttered. He wasn't going to tell her. Maggie knew he wasn't, and she got good and mad.

"You're *exactly* like him," she said, pulling her hand away. "Too damned bottled up to share even the tiniest piece of yourself." She wanted to hit him, so she moved away to avoid the temptation, scooping up the Data Tech report and hugging it close to her chest as she sat in the farthest possible corner of the tiny closet. She glared at him. "Well, guess what, Charlie boy? I'm probably going to die for you tomorrow, for the *second* time around. You can at least show me the courtesy of answering my questions!"

The shuttered look was replaced by shock. "The *second* time . . . ?"

"I already took a bullet for you," she told him flatly. "Seven years from now. Only this time around, it's probably going to happen tomorrow. The least you could do is *talk* to me and tell me why I'm going to die."

He was struggling to understand. "You knew you'd already been killed once, and you still stuck around to help Chuck? To help . . . me?"

Maggie tipped her head back against the wall and closed her eyes. "Yeah, love's a funny thing, isn't it, Charlie? I'm in love with Chuck." She opened her eyes and looked at him. "And I love you too. You're him, you know. Part of you is Chuck—except for the fact that you don't happen to love me." She laughed, but it came out sounding more like a sob. "How could you love me? You don't know me. But just think, if I had seven years, I could probably make you love me as much as Chuck does. Of course, it would probably take another seven years *more* for you ever to admit it!"

Charles was silent.

"Please," Maggie said. "Give me something. Close your eyes and find that part of you that could maybe love me in seven years. And then tell me why finding a way to travel through time has ruled your life since you were a child."

Charles didn't move. He didn't even blink.

Maggie closed her eyes again. She couldn't bear to look at him as she waited for him to say something, anything. Or nothing at all.

He cleared his throat. "I've . . . I've never told anyone."

He was either going to keep going, or he was going to stop. Maggie sat absolutely still, waiting to see which it was going to be.

Charles cleared his throat again. "When I was seven years old, I . . . um, I realized that life was made up of linear paths. If you took one, you missed the others, and . . . vice versa."

He paused, and she knew he was struggling to simplify, to make his words ones she would understand. "It occurred to me that all along these lines or paths were these . . . moments. Moments in time that either kept a person on track or pushed them onto a totally different path. Sometimes these moments—or decisions, if you will—seem utterly trivial, but the changes they trigger are . . . immense."

He took a deep breath. "From everything you've told me, it seems as if my decision to continue or to stop trying to make a working theorem for time travel is one of these moments. Quiet. Seemingly insignificant. Yet from everything you told me—the bomb at the White House, Wizard-9's interference, your own death—" His voice broke and he stopped for a moment.

Maggie opened her eyes and looked at him. He was staring down at his stockinged feet, his eyes out of focus, his jaw clenched, mouth grim. He looked up and met her gaze. "It seems the changes this decision will bring are extremely severe—unless we can somehow alter the path again and take us all in an entirely different direction. Unless . . ." He looked away from her, his eyes narrowing in concentration as he became lost in his thoughts.

"What happened when you were seven, Chuck?" she said softly, gently. Chuck. She'd gone and called him Chuck. The name had slipped out.

Her mistake hadn't gotten past him. She saw his awareness in the flash of his eyes, in the slight twisting of his lips into a half smile.

He didn't want to tell her. He shifted his position. He ran his fingers through his hair. He looked at the walls in the closet, the floor, the ceiling. He chewed on the inside of his cheek. He scratched his ear. He stopped himself more than once from drumming his fingers on the floor.

"Another moment," he finally said through clenched teeth, glancing briefly at her. "It was another one of those goddammed life-altering moments."

Maggie moved so that she was sitting directly across from him. She stretched out her right leg so that her bare foot was resting directly on top of Charles's left foot. The physical contact seemed to ground him, and for a moment he just sat there, eyes closed, absolutely still, as if gaining strength from her touch.

"I was reading a book." His voice was so soft, Maggie wasn't sure at first that he'd really spoken. "*The Lord of the Rings.* J.R.R. Tolkien. I was three chapters from the end, and I didn't want to put it down."

He paused, and Maggie held her breath as she realized that his eyes were shining with unshed tears.

"My little brother," he said. "Steven. He came into my room. He wanted to play Chinese checkers. But I only had a half hour before my calculus tutor arrived, and I wanted to read, so I told him no. I couldn't play with him. I didn't even look up from my book to talk to him—I just told him to shut the door on his way out, and he did. About twenty minutes later I heard sirens and then Danny MacAllister, the kid from down the street who delivered the newspapers, he pounded on our front door, and God, it was Stevie. The sirens were for Stevie. He was riding his new bike, crossing New Amsterdam Road, and he got hit by a truck. He was killed instantly."

ELEVEN

"Oh, Charles, no," Maggie breathed.

"I don't know what he was doing. He wasn't supposed to ride his bike anywhere but around the cul-de-sac. He must've been mad at me—" He broke off.

"I don't know what he was doing," he said again, softer this time. "I never knew why he did the things he did. He was so emotional. So . . . illogical. He was five, and he couldn't even read Dr. Seuss yet. He wasn't 'gifted,' but he didn't care—he was just this happy little silly kid. Everyone loved him, especially me. Everything was so easy for him. My father would play catch and laugh with him out in the backyard, and then come inside and shake his head at me for making careless errors in my calculus assignments."

Now that he was finally talking, the words seemed to spill out. "I used to sneak into Stevie's room at night and climb into his top bunk and ask him what he was thinking about, and he would say something like duckies or bunnies, and I would lie there and try to *be* him. I'd make shadows on the walls with my fingers, the way he did, and I'd try to push aside all the numbers and physics equations in my head to make a little room for duckies and bunnies." Charles laughed, a short burst of not very humorous air. "But I never really could."

Maggie's heart was in her throat. She could picture Charles—Chuck—as that terribly intelligent and gifted child, with eyes far too old and sober for his skinny, seven-year-old face and body.

"And just like that, Stevie was gone," he continued. "One game of Chinese checkers. That's all it would have taken to keep our entire family from being destroyed. But I wouldn't play, and my brother died."

His voice broke, and he stopped, turning away from her so that she wouldn't see the sheen of tears in his eyes that threatened to overflow.

"It wasn't your fault," she said, moving closer, wanting to reach for him but afraid of being pushed away. "Didn't your mother and father tell you that?"

"My father left town," he said, his voice curiously flat. He held himself away from her, his shoulders stiff. But try as he might, he couldn't stop the tears that flooded his eyes. One escaped, and he brusquely, almost savagely wiped it away. "I never saw him again. And my mother . . . She lost it. Literally. She went into a hospital and wouldn't get out of bed. She died about four months later. They wouldn't tell me what she died of— I've always assumed she managed to give herself some kind of overdose of sleeping pills."

"Oh, Charles." Maggie was aghast at the avalanche of tragedies that had begun with his brother's death. "What happened to you? Who took care of *you*?"

"I was sent to live with my mother's elderly uncle in New York."

"That was where the housekeeper made you carrot cake," Maggie realized. "And you ate it even though you hated it."

Somehow it was that image, the image of a little boy choking down something that was meant to be a treat, that pushed Maggie over the edge. She reached for Charles, wishing that she could hold that little boy in her arms.

He resisted her for only a second, and then he turned and held her just as tightly.

His parents had deserted him at a time when he'd needed them the most. They had selfishly given in to their own pain and grief, leaving no one to hold and comfort their surviving son. Had anyone ever held him? Maggie wondered. Had anyone told him it was all right to cry, that it was necessary to grieve?

He'd been hardly more than a baby himself—only seven years old. He may have been capable of college-level mathematics, but he had been only a *child*.

Maggie could picture him, all alone in his uncle's quiet house, sitting in his room, thinking that if only he could turn back time and tell his brother, yes, he'd play that game of Chinese checkers . . .

"If I could go back in time," she whispered, stroking his hair, his back. "I'd go back to find you. And I would hold you, just like this, and I would tell you that it *wasn't* your fault. I would tell you that's it's okay to cry—that you *need* to cry. And I would make sure you knew that someone loved you . . . that *I* love you."

He drew in a ragged breath as his arms tightened

around her, as he pulled back to look down at her. His cheeks were wet with tears. "I sure could've used you."

"I would've told you to look at me." Maggie gazed up into his eyes, gently touching the side of his face. "To remember me. And to wait for me to show up in your life again. And I would have told you that the next time you see me, I would be there for you—forever. That no matter the mistakes you think you've made, no matter what you hold yourself responsible for, no matter whether you stay at Data Tech or go back to medical school or get a job washing cars, I'll still love you. I'll always love you. And that, from that moment on, from that moment when we meet again"—her voice trembled slightly—"the only thing that can part us is death."

Charles gazed down at the woman in his arms, knowing without a doubt that her words were not meant only for the little boy he had once been. Her words were aimed just as well at him, and also at the man he would become.

What a powerful thing this love that she had for him was! Without any intricate equations, without any high-tech equipment, without any help from science at all, her love could travel through time and touch the child he had once been, the man he was, and the man he would become. With that love, she could soothe and start to heal wounds that had festered for too long.

And he could look into the warmth and compassion of this woman's beautiful eyes and feel a peacefulness that he hadn't felt in years.

But he felt a yearning too. He wanted her now, not seven years from now. He wanted to pull her chin up and lower his mouth to hers and . . .

As if she somehow was able to read his mind, Maggie brushed her lips across his.

It took everything he had in him not to pull her closer, not to catch her mouth with his and deepen that soft kiss. God, how easy it would be to love her. The depth of her feelings for him was astonishing. He wanted to take that love and keep it all to himself, all *for* himself.

But he knew that everything she said to him was said to Chuck as well. And every kiss she gave him was a kiss Chuck would remember. Charles was merely a transmitter, a medium connecting her to his future self—to the man she really loved.

Still, when she kissed him again, when the sweetness of her lips lingered against his, he couldn't help himself. He gave in to the temptation and kissed her hungrily, greedily, taking what she offered and then some, plundering the softness of her mouth.

And when she tugged him down with her onto the carpeted closet floor, he could no longer resist. He gave up trying to fight as she pulled her shirt—*his* shirt—over her head, as he filled his hands with her soft breasts, as he touched her silky skin.

She pulled back slightly to smile into his eyes. It was a tremulous smile, barely able to hide the tears that hovered so close to the surface.

But she didn't stop. She unfastened his pants, and he knew if he let her, unless he stopped her, they would make love—right here, right now.

He didn't want to stop her. He couldn't have stopped her if he'd tried. He knew she saw Chuck when she looked into his eyes. He knew she kissed Chuck when she kissed his lips. And when she slipped her panties down her legs, when she helped him pull his own pants down, when she straddled him, surrounding him in one swift, incredible moment with her slick heat, he knew it was Chuck she was loving so completely.

He wished he were wrong. He wished she saw him, really saw *him* as she looked deeply into his eyes, as she moved on top of him.

The sensations he felt were unlike anything he'd ever experienced before, but he knew despite that, it could be even better. It would be a thousand times better if he were the one she truly wanted, if he were the one she really loved.

She moved faster now, each stroke driving him closer and closer to release. Closer and closer to . . .

He caught her hips, trying to still her movement. "Maggie, I'm not wearing a condom. . . ."

Maggie kissed him. "Charlie, there's a really good chance I'm going to die tomorrow. I think that's just cause for irresponsible behavior. Because I don't know if you noticed, but I seem to have lost my handbag, and I'm currently not equipped with any pockets. . . ."

He smiled, sliding his hands down her naked body. "I did happen to notice your lack of pockets." He lifted her off of him, shifting slightly as he reached underneath him, searching for something. "But I have pockets *and* my wallet, and . . ." He tore open the foil packet. "A condom."

"I honestly don't think it matters."

He looked up at her, and his dark eyes were so serious. "I'm not going to let you die." He actually believed his own words.

Maggie couldn't be so certain. All she knew, all she was absolutely positive about was how much she truly loved this man. The line between Charles and Chuck had long since blurred. It had been all but erased as Charles had told her so poignantly about his little brother.

True, she'd damn near had to throttle the story out of him. But he *had* told her. And he'd told her far, far more than Chuck ever would have. Chuck would've finally revealed the cold facts surrounding his family's tragedy. But to talk about his love for the little boy, to express his yearning to live as uncomplicated and carefree a life as Steven had . . . Chuck, with his well-practiced control would never have shared that much of himself.

But Charles had.

She kissed him, loving the way his eyes lit with fire as she pressed herself down on top of him again, as he filled her so completely.

She loved him. Charles, Chuck, the grieving, lonely seven-year-old boy he had once been—she loved them all. Chuck was right all along—he and Charles *were* the same man.

And this moment, this short time they had, locked here together in this tiny closet, might be the only time she had left to share with him.

She didn't care about the fact that at any moment Ken Goodwin or one of the other Wizard-9 agents might unlock the bolts and open the door. She didn't care about anything.

Except for showing this man exactly how he made her feel.

He kissed her, lifting her up and lowering her down so that she was on her back. She knew just where to touch him, just what he liked, and she saw awareness and a certain vulnerability in his eyes. This may have been his first time with her, but she had been with him before.

She gazed up at him as he set a rhythm that made her blood burn, looking again for that softness in his eyes, praying that for him this was not just a flare-up of lust between two near strangers.

He smiled down at her, an echo of Chuck's tentative, crooked smile. But again, his eyes revealed far more than Chuck's eyes ever would. There *was* more to this for him than sex—she could see it in his eyes.

She pulled his head down and kissed him, claiming his mouth as possessively as he claimed her body. She heard him groan, felt his body tense, and she knew he was as close to his release as she.

She clung to him, holding him tightly, pulling him even closer, wanting to feel as much of him against as much of her as she possibly could, wanting truly to become one.

And then, with an explosion of sensation, with a flare of pleasure so intense, all lines and boundaries between them vanished as they *did* become one. Maggie couldn't tell where she ended and Charles began as they spun together, out of this dimension and into a place where time stood still. There was only the scorching ecstasy of shared release. The sweet joy of complete communion.

Then they sighed—he did. Or maybe she did. Or perhaps they both did. Together, separately, it didn't matter—as slowly they drifted back to earth. Slowly, the sensation of his arms around her, of his weight on top of her, his hair tickling her nose broke through. Slowly, awareness returned. She could feel the carpet beneath her, see spiderwebs up in the corners of the closet ceiling.

Then Charles lifted his head, and she found herself gazing into his eyes. He looked at her searchingly, as if uncertain of her response to what they'd just done.

She smiled at him, running her fingers through the softness of his hair. "I sure am glad I didn't drown today. I really would've hated to miss that."

His face relaxed into a hot, quick smile. "I'm glad too. More than you can imagine." He kissed her hard on the mouth. "You want to get out of here?"

Maggie froze. "You're going to do it? You're going to decide to give up your research?"

He pulled himself off of her, helping her up and handing her his shirt as he quickly found his own pants. He'd turned away, but not before Maggie saw the answer to her questions in his eyes.

No. He wasn't going to quit. Maggie didn't know whether to feel frustrated or relieved.

"You have the power to end this once and for all," she told him as she fumbled with the buttons on the shirt.

"I can't do it," he told her, his voice low. "All my life I've wanted to go back. To save him. I can't just give it up. Not without trying to find another way."

"You don't think Chuck has tried to find another way?"

He glanced at her, his eyes apologetic. "I think that I can't just quit before I have a chance to talk to him.

What if together we can come up with a solution that neither of us would have thought of alone?"

"What if you do something to get yourself killed?" she countered.

"Ken Goodwin's not going to risk—"

"Accidents can happen, Charlie. What if they go for me and this time *you* step in the way of the bullet?"

He tried to make light of it. "Then I guess there'll be no Wells Project."

Maggie wasn't amused. "If you're dead, Chuck will be dead too."

Charles was quiet as he slipped his shoes back onto his feet. "Believe me, I'll do my best to make sure both he and I survive," he finally said.

"So how exactly do you plan to get us not only out of this closet but also off this ranch?" Maggie asked. "I'm particularly curious as to how you intend to keep the Wizard-9 agents and their hired guns from shooting great big holes in me as we wave good-bye, driving . . . which car, Charles? We seem to have left ours back in the Data Tech parking lot."

"We'll take one of their cars."

"Wait, don't tell me. You'll hot-wire it, right?"

"No, I'll have them give me the keys. We'll get out of here faster that way." He picked up the rope from the closet floor—the two lengths of rope that had bound her hands and feet. "Here's what we're going to do."

"Are you ready?" Maggie asked. She'd put her dress back on. It was cold and wet and she shivered slightly.

Charles nodded. With his help, she'd managed to

tear the bottom few feet of fabric off the dress, shortening it so it didn't go down much past her knees. That would help when it came time to run. "Remember, when they start opening the locks, step back behind me, and stay down."

"But be ready to move fast," she said, repeating his instructions. "And stay close to you at all times. I know." She glanced around the tiny closet, down at the Wells Project report still lying on the rug. She kicked it with her toe. "All this trouble over a bunch of equations."

As Maggie looked back up at Charles, he saw through her bravado. Her eyes were so wide, her face so pale. "Charlie, if this doesn't work—"

"I'm not going to let them hurt you."

"I know that's what you intend—"

"I *promise*."

She kissed him. He could taste her fear. Or maybe it was his own. "I love you."

Charles nodded, forcing a smile. He had no doubt in his mind that Chuck already knew that. "Come on, Maggie, let's get this done."

She took a deep breath. "Okay, I'm ready." Squaring her shoulders, she approached the door. Another deep breath, and then she was pounding on it. Pounding and shouting as if the world were coming to an end. "Help! Somebody help me please! Charles is trying to *hang* himself! He won't let me near him, and I'm afraid he's going to die!"

She kept it up, shouting and banging, pounding and shrieking until there it was, the sound of the bolts on the outside of the door being thrown.

As Charles braced himself Maggie scrambled toward

the back of the closet. The door was pulled open, and one of the Wizard-9 agents—the hulking man Charles had had his wrestling match with earlier that day—got a glimpse of him, rope tied around his neck, lashed so that it looked as if he were hanging from the closet pole.

It was true that he had to bend his knees and lift his feet off the ground, which had to look rather ridiculous. And it was also true that the pole wasn't going to hold his weight for more than another few seconds. But a few seconds was all he needed as the Wizard-9 agent rushed forward to rescue him.

Charles released the rope as soon as the hulk was close enough to reach for him, and his sudden unexpected body weight was enough to take the man down. They collapsed together onto the closet floor and Charles had his hands on the man's gun as he kneed him sharply in the groin—all before the other Wizard-9 agents standing in the doorway even realized what was happening.

The hulk was writhing as Charles scrambled to his feet, gun in hand. He could feel Maggie next to him, pressed against his back just as he'd told her. He pointed the gun at the other agents as everything around him seemed to switch into slow motion.

"Hands up!" he shouted, moving forward, pushing them back out of the closet. If they didn't respond to the threat to themselves, he'd point the gun at himself—see how quickly they'd react to the possibility of his ending the Wells Project before it began by way of his own untimely death.

He was banking on the fact that they wouldn't call his bluff.

And then, from the other side of the house, came the unmistakable sound of gunfire. It was the rapid-fire sound of an automatic weapon, and from the way Maggie's hands tightened on his arms, he knew she'd come to the same conclusion he had.

Chuck was here.

But was he on the giving or receiving end of those gunshots?

Before Charles could take so much as a step toward the door, an explosion rocked the foundation of the house. He realized as he looked out the windows that more time had gone by than he'd realized. It was evening. The sky was dark.

He motioned toward the Wizard-9 agents again with his gun. "Drop your weapons."

But before anyone moved, the door to the room was kicked open, and there in the hallway stood . . . himself.

He was dressed all in black. Black jeans, black boots, black turtleneck shirt. His face was camouflaged with smears of grease and dirt, and he was holding the kind of assault weapon Boyd Rogers used in his adventures as a Navy SEAL. He was holding it as if he knew how to use it, and use it well.

Charles stared for a fraction of a second into his own eyes. Into *Chuck*'s eyes. The man he would become in seven years. The man Maggie loved.

"Get down!" Chuck shouted, and Charles turned to see the two Wizard-9 agents hadn't dropped their weapons when he'd told them to. And still in that same slow motion, he saw them turn and aim their guns at Chuck.

Charles pulled Maggie away, pushing her onto the

floor behind a big double bed. He heard the sound of Chuck's gun, heard Maggie scream, and he tried to cover her more completely with his body. There was the sound of shouting voices, more gunshots, then silence.

And then there was the sound of his own voice—Chuck's voice—saying, "You better get moving. The east wing of the house is on fire. It's dry as hell—it's not going to be long before this whole place goes up."

Charles pulled himself to his feet. And found himself gazing down at the earthly remains of three Wizard-9 agents.

He heard Maggie's swift intake of air, and he pulled her away from the sight. "Don't look," he told her, pushing her toward the door.

Chuck was sitting on the floor, leaning against the wall, his gun cradled in his arms, as if the fact that he'd just snuffed out three lives meant nothing to him.

Maggie ran to him, and Charles felt a sharp flare of jealousy that he tried to stifle. She'd been nothing but honest with him. He'd known all along, even while they were making love, that Chuck owned her heart.

But he didn't have to watch as Maggie threw herself into Chuck's arms. He didn't have to watch as she kissed him. Because she didn't. Instead, she knelt beside him on the floor and turned to look up at Charles.

"Charlie, he's been hit!"

Only then did Charles see the smear of blood on the white wall. Chuck's blood. *His* blood.

"I should have remembered the man in the closet," Chuck said through tightly clenched teeth. "But I didn't, and he surprised me."

"But I had his gun—"

"You had *one* of his guns."

"It's his right leg," Maggie told him as he crouched beside her.

Chuck held out his gun to Charles. "Here. Take this and go with Maggie. Quickly."

TWELVE

"We're not going anywhere without you," Maggie said fiercely. She turned to look at Charles. "How bad is it?"

Chuck answered. "It's not bad, but I won't be able to run. I don't think I can even walk."

"I'll carry the gun, you carry him," Maggie said to Charles.

"No, I'll slow you down—"

"So?"

Chuck's eyes blazed. "So I may have taken care of the others and destroyed the Runabout, but Goodwin got away. He could be anywhere. And I know for damn sure that he's going to be aiming his gun at *you*, Maggie. You need to be able to move, and move *fast*."

Chuck had "taken care of" the other Wizard-9 agents. That's what he called shooting them full of bullets and draining the life from them. Maggie kept her back firmly turned to the sight of the three dead men sprawled on the other side of the room. How could he be so matter-of-fact, so emotionless about killing? How many times in the past had he been forced to kill? Or had he always been so callous and thick-skinned?

She risked a glance at Charles. His expression was grimly identical to Chuck's. Maybe he didn't care. Maybe the thought of those three men never standing up and going home to their wives and children didn't make him sick to his stomach, either.

"Maggie's the only reason I'd risk building another Runabout," Chuck said, his voice harsh. She looked up at him and she could see pain mixed in with the fiery intensity in his eyes. His wound may not have been "bad," but it hurt him badly.

"And Ken Goodwin knows that," he continued. "If you're dead, Mags, I'd keep my theories of time travel alive." He thrust his gun at Charles. "Come on, kid. I'm expendable. I'll be gone anyway when you finally do the right thing and decide to leave Data Tech. So take it and get Maggie the hell out of here."

"You *did* know," Maggie interrupted. "You knew all along that if I could convince Charles to give up his research, you'd just disappear, didn't you? I can't believe you would let yourself vanish without saying good-bye!"

"I did say good-bye," he said quietly.

Her voice caught. "You didn't mention that that good-bye was because you intended to leave me forever."

Chuck's gaze flickered to Charles, who was quietly working to stanch the flow of his blood. "My intention was to never leave you again."

"You mean your intention was for *Charles* to never leave me again." Charles glanced uneasily over at her, and she shook her head. "Don't worry, Charlie, I won't hold you to any promises you made seven years in the future."

Charles straightened up, picking up Chuck's gun and handing it back to him. "Let's go," he said.

Chuck pushed the gun back toward him. "No."

"We're not leaving you here," Charles stated.

"Instead you'd rather risk Maggie's life?" Chuck countered.

Charles glanced back at the dead Wizard-9 agents. "I think we'd be risking Maggie's life if we left you here," he said quietly. He hefted the weight of Chuck's gun. "Because I don't think I could bring myself to use this the way you can."

"Believe me, you'd use it. If Goodwin pointed his gun at her, you could bring yourself to use it," Chuck told Charles.

"Yeah," Charles agreed. "Maybe I could. But I'd rather not have to find out." He glanced back at the bodies again, the muscles clenching in his jaw. "That's one way I have absolutely no desire to be like you, old man."

"Please, can we go now?" Maggie whispered. "*All* of us?"

Chuck let Charles help him to his feet, swearing sharply, his mouth tight against the pain. He took back the gun, holding it at the ready in one arm while Charles pulled his other arm around his neck. But he also drew his handgun, the small one he'd bought illegally in the roadhouse north of Phoenix, and held it out to Charles.

Charles took it unwillingly, jamming it down into the pocket of his torn tuxedo jacket.

Chuck gritted his teeth. "Let's do it, then."

Both men spoke in unison. "Maggie, get behind me."

Charles proved to be as good as Chuck when it came to taking precautions and evading capture.

He got them into one of the Wizard-9 limousines, and they'd pulled away from the burning ranch house, the flames from the fire cracking and dancing, lighting up the night behind them. They'd hit the gate going fifty, and the big car had plowed right through.

Charles had driven directly down the mountain and into Phoenix, where they quickly left the limo on a side street. The danger and Chuck's injury made borrowing another car a necessity, although Maggie kept careful track of each of the streets from which they purloined yet another vehicle. After this was over, she'd go back and make retribution.

If she were alive.

Charles knew the same trick with switching license plates that Chuck had pulled not so many nights ago. He drove them from one side of Phoenix to the other, making sure they weren't being followed before he shut off the car's headlights and pulled into the driveway of a house that was dark and silent.

"Where are we?" Maggie asked. The neighborhood was upscale suburban, complete with thick green grass growing on every lawn. In the somewhat cooler darkness of the night, sprinkler systems were going full blast in the yards all around them. She could just imagine the water bills.

"A vice-president from Data Tech is out of town,"

Charles told her. "He's in Ireland with his family until next week."

"You mean Randy Lowenstein? If it's Randy, we're not safe here. Goodwin will have access to the schedules of all my—your—friends," Chuck said warningly from the backseat. His voice sounded tight. Maggie could only imagine the pain he'd endured during the course of the night.

"This isn't Randy's house. It's Harmon Gregory's, VP of finance. He's not a friend," Charles said quietly. "In fact, I only met him once, when Randy and I delivered something here to his house. I overheard Gregory's secretary talking to mine, heard her mention Ireland." He turned around to look at Chuck over the back of the seat. "Do you still carry a Swiss army knife? Goodwin's men took mine."

Silently, Chuck handed his pocketknife to Charles, who pulled up the parking brake and climbed out of the car.

Maggie turned to look at Chuck.

In the backseat, his face was completely in shadows.

"Are you sure we shouldn't take you to a hospital?"

"I have a bullet in my leg," he said. "They'd have to notify the police."

"How are we going to get the bullet out? What if it gets infected? I don't want you to die." Her voice cracked softly.

He was silent, unmoving. When he finally spoke, his voice was raspy, and he had to stop to clear his throat. "I'm not going to be here long enough to need to get the bullet out."

"But you said you destroyed the Runabout. Can't you just—"

"I did, and although the time pressures are off, that doesn't mean we can just pretend the threat's not still here. We need to convince . . . Charlie . . . to quit his research. I still need your help, Mags."

"Isn't there any other way?"

"No." The word held all of his absolute resolve, but he said it gently.

"How can you be sure? Maybe if you talked to Charles, together you might—"

"Maggie, do you think I haven't tried to find some loophole, some alternative—" He broke off, intentionally taking a deep breath and lowering his voice again. "Here's what we'd need to do. We'd need to hunt down and kill Ken Goodwin. And then we'd need to hunt down and kill his present-day counterpart, because what if, God forbid, he got in touch with himself and tipped himself off as to what you and I did at the Data Tech lab that day. But then, you know, I'd start wondering about the other members of the Wizard-9 organization. Maybe he'd told them. We'd have to kill them, too, wouldn't we?"

"All right," she said.

But he didn't stop. "Or how about Goodwin's wife? Maybe he told her. Should we kill her too? And his children . . . ?"

"Stop." Her voice was only a whisper, but he heard her.

"I'm sorry."

Maggie blinked back tears as she looked out the windshield at Charles. He was working with Chuck's

Swiss army knife, doing something to the small key plat
on the frame of the garage door.

"I saw your face after I killed those men." Chuc
spoke almost inaudibly. "I can do it when I have to
Maggie. But I'm not going to kill everyone that Ke
Goodwin might've talked to. I can't do that. Even if yo
wanted me to, I couldn't. But I know you don't want m
to. What I've already done is bad enough for you."

Silence. Outside, Charles made an adjustment wit
the knife and the automatic garage door slid up.

He quickly began refastening the key panel to th
frame.

"Will you help me?"

Maggie closed her eyes for a moment. "Yes."

Chuck touched her then, reaching forward, leanin
out of the darkness to squeeze her shoulder. "Than
you."

She turned to face him, catching his hand in hers
keeping him from disappearing once again into th
shadows.

"I love . . . both of you." She felt tears welling u
in her eyes again.

His face looked so tired, his eyes so filled with pain
"There's really only one of us. There *will* be only one o
us."

And that one wasn't going to be the man sitting fac
ing her, gazing into her eyes.

He reached forward and caught one of her tears wit
his finger. "That's a *good* thing. It's going to be a goo
thing." He touched her cheek, her hair. "Hey," he said
"you don't think I *like* what I've become, do you? Always
having to look over my shoulder, always suspicious

ready to kill or be killed . . . ? This way I get a second chance, Mags. I can take a do-over. Not many people get that kind of opportunity." His eyes softened as she pressed her cheek into his hand. "It's not like you're never going to see me again. You will. I promise. I'm going to be a little different—no, a whole lot different, probably. *Better* different." He smiled. "But you'll see me again, and I'll kiss you"—he leaned forward and brushed her lips with his—"just like that, and you'll look into my eyes and you'll know it's me. I'll remember everything. Very faintly, but I *will* remember."

Charles opened the door of the car, and the sudden light seemed blinding. Chuck sat back, letting go of Maggie's hand as Charles climbed behind the steering wheel.

"I'm sorry," Charles said quietly as he shut the door and the car was plunged once more into darkness. "I didn't mean to interrupt."

He quickly pulled the car into the empty garage and shut off the engine. He got out of the car just as quickly, and using one of the buttons near the door to the house, he lowered the automatic garage door.

They were hidden.

At least for now.

Charles was in Data Tech VP Harmon Gregory's living room, sitting in the dark. They didn't dare turn on any lights. Although the houses in this wealthy suburb were quite a distance apart, he didn't want anyone seeing lights on in a house that was supposed to be empty.

He was sitting with his head back and his eyes closed.

He was trying to push aside his exhaustion so that he could think, when he heard a radio switched on from somewhere in the back of the house.

He stood up and moved swiftly down the hall toward the bedrooms.

Maggie was in one of those rooms, in the dark, putting plastic trash bags underneath the bed linens to keep the Gregorys' mattress from being stained by Chuck's blood. Chuck was in the bathroom, with the only candle they'd found, trying his best to clean himself up—something he'd insisted upon doing on his own. Charles could hear the water running behind the closed door.

He came face-to-face with Maggie in the hallway as she, too, heard the radio. He tried not to think about the way he'd seen her, sitting in the car, her eyes filled with tears, holding desperately to Chuck's hand as he kissed her. He tried, and failed.

"Is someone here?" she breathed, her eyes wide.

Charles put one finger to his lips and moved forward, trying to see into the room where the radio played. He could make out the shape of the bed and . . .

It was empty.

From the other side of the window shades, he could see the first light of dawn streaking across the morning sky.

"It's a clock radio," he said, crossing the room and raising one of the shades an inch, letting in a little more of the early-morning light. The room was that of a teenage girl, with magazine pictures and posters plastered over the walls. A bright yellow bedspread covered a bed that was littered with a menagerie of tiny stuffed animals.

Maggie was staring down at the radio, a slight frown wrinkling her forehead. "That song . . ."

The melody of the slow pop ballad was hauntingly familiar despite the fact that Charles couldn't remember the last time he'd listened to a Top 40 radio station.

Maggie looked up at him. "We danced to this song at the Data Tech party. Do you remember?"

He did. He remembered it now too. Faintly. Foggily. As if remembering a dream. And it had to be a dream—neither of them had gone to the Data Tech party.

Maggie laughed. "It's a residual memory," she said. "We're remembering things that happened the first time around. Wow, I've never had one this vivid."

That had to be what it was. And she was right. It *was* vivid. Although it was misty, he saw the events played out as if he were remembering a scene from a movie. As if he were *living* a movie. "I saw you from across the lobby," Charles recalled, "and followed you into the dining room. I was determined to find someone who could introduce us—" He broke off, shaking his head in confusion. "But we'd already met, in the restaurant."

"No, we hadn't met before," Maggie told him. "Not the first time. You just came up to me, introduced yourself, and asked me to dance."

"You said yes. I was thrilled." Charles pulled her into his arms and began to dance with her, as if they were there, right now, at the Data Tech party.

"You were very charming," Maggie remembered, tilting her head to look up at him. "I think we talked until midnight. I told you my entire life story—about growing up in Connecticut and coming out to Arizona State U. and ending up in Phoenix—and it wasn't until I got home that I realized you'd told me next to nothing about yourself."

"I wanted to kiss you while we were dancing, but we were surrounded by people we both worked with, so I asked you to have dinner with me the next night instead."

"I agreed to meet you at Tia's."

"A Mexican restaurant near your house?"

"Yeah." Maggie smiled up at him.

"You were late."

"A client called just as I was going out the door."

"When you arrived I remember thinking it was like being hit by a hurricane. You had so much energy. You must've apologized twenty times."

"I was afraid you might've gotten tired of waiting. I was afraid you'd left. I was so glad to see you."

Charles pushed her hair back from her face. They'd long since stopped dancing, but he still held her in his arms. "You called me Chuck."

She nodded, her smile fading. "I know."

"You said I needed a nickname."

"You said you didn't care *what* I called you—"

Charles smiled. "So you started calling me Frank—until I retracted my statement." He touched her lips gently with his thumb, tracing them. "All I could think about all night long was how badly I wanted to kiss you."

"All *I* could think about was how much I wanted you to tell me about yourself. I'd pretty much decided that if I could get you to open up to me, I'd let you walk me home, and I'd even . . . invite you to stay."

Invite him to . . . His arms tightened around her. "Oh God. Really?"

Maggie shook her head, smiling almost shyly up at him. "I liked you a lot. Right from the start. But I wanted you to *talk* to me. I tried, but you sidestepped all my questions."

"I knew you wanted something more from me," he said quietly, "but I don't—I didn't—feel comfortable talking about myself, about my past."

"I would've settled for you telling me how you felt."

"I felt happy. You made me smile, made me feel so warm. And hot. God, I've never wanted a woman the way I wanted you—the way I still want you. I had this feeling that you were going to walk away from me," Charles whispered. "But I still couldn't give you what you needed."

"You gave me what I needed today." Maggie reached up to touch him. "Was it really that hard to talk to me?"

"No." He closed his eyes, loving the sensation of her fingers in his hair. "Yes."

She laughed, and feeling a burst of that now familiar warmth and heat, he lowered his head to kiss her. But she stopped him.

"You didn't want to talk about your brother's death, but you've never let yourself forget or move forward, away from it," Maggie pointed out. "Even now. You're still tied to what happened when you were a child." Her eyes were so serious as she gazed up at him. "After all this time Stevie's life is still more important to you than your own."

Charles didn't speak. What could he possibly say?

The sound of the bathroom door opening made him step back, away from her. He hadn't liked watching

Chuck with Maggie in the car. The least he could do was spare his future self a similar sight.

Maggie moved toward the door. "I better finish fixing the sheets."

"I'll do it," Charles said, turning off the radio. "I'd like a chance to talk to him. Privately. If you don't mind."

"Of course I don't mind."

Chuck appeared in the hallway, holding on to the frame of the door, propelling himself forward by hopping on his good leg. He was unable to keep from watching Maggie as she quietly came down the hall and moved past him.

Charles could read so much in the darkness of the other man's eyes. Did his own feelings and hunger for Maggie show so clearly in his own eyes?

"I'll be in the living room if you need me," Maggie turned back to say.

What did she see when she saw them standing there together like this? Did they look as different as Charles imagined? Did he seem like a mere shadow of his older, more experienced self? Did he pale so utterly in comparison?

Pushing his troublesome thoughts away, Charles helped Chuck into the bedroom. Chuck had already hung the strap of his assault weapon over one of the bedposts, and he checked, making sure it was within reach as Charles helped him into the bed.

"You know, for the past few years," Chuck said, breaking the silence, "ever since the news about the Wells Project was leaked to the public, I haven't gone anywhere without a matched pair of bodyguards. My house—your house—was turned into a fortress. I put in a security system that kept the world out." His voice got softer. "And kept me locked in."

Chuck leaned over, opening the drawers of a small bedside table one at a time, gritting his teeth against the pain in his leg.

"I know what you're trying to do—"

"Let me finish," Chuck interrupted as he pulled a gleaming wooden box from one of the drawers. "I figured old Harmon Gregory might have one of these."

"Have one of what?"

"It's not even locked. And this man has *kids*." Chuck flipped open the box to reveal a shining silver handgun. "It's loaded too. Son of a bitch." He took the gun, then put the box back in the drawer, pushing it closed.

"Over the past few years," he told Charles as he hefted that small but dangerous-looking weapon, "I've had to carry a gun, and I've had to use it. More times than I like to remember. That's your destiny—if you continue to pursue the Wells Project."

He set the gun down on top of the bedside table, well within his reach.

"I just don't see how you can expect me to let the Wells Project go." Charles started to pace. "I don't see how *you* could just let it go. All my life, I've wanted— *we've* wanted—to travel back through time. To fix things that went wrong. To save Stevie. Have you forgotten?"

"Look at me closely, Charlie. I'm your own personal ghost of Christmas future. Look into my eyes, really look, and see what you have to look forward to if you continue on your current path. I've seen a good friend killed. Boyd Rogers."

Charles stopped pacing.

"You didn't know about Boyd, huh, Charlie boy? Well, he died on this path that leads from you to me. And Maggie too. Do you really want to find out what it feels like to have the woman you care more about than anything else in the world die in your arms?"

Charles was silent. He couldn't answer.

"Look at me," Chuck commanded him harshly. "I'm a dead man. I have no future. And it was my obsession to change my past, my refusal to reconcile myself with Stevie's death, that's led me right here. *Right* here."

Charles took a deep breath. "I realize that there are difficulties to overcome," he said, "but surely there's a way to keep Maggie and Boyd safe, to prevent the Wizard-9 agents from using the Runabout to plant that bomb in the White House, *and* still have access to time travel. All we need to do is to think it through—"

"There's not." Chuck leaned his head wearily back against the pillows. "You know, I had plenty of chances to go back and save Stevie, but I didn't. It was one thing to dream about it, but another to actually do it. I realized that I would risk totally changing history."

"By saving the life of one five-year-old boy?"

"Absolutely." Chuck sat up again. "Did you know that the trucker who killed him was driving drunk? Did you know that he went to jail for vehicular manslaughter? If he hadn't been stopped, God only knows who he might've killed either later that afternoon or some other day. He might've killed someone who grew up to play some tiny, stupid, but vitally important part in world history. He might've killed the boy or girl who was destined to grow up to be a mechanic, that due to his or her shoddy work made a car break down before it could get into an accident and kill someone *else*—someone destined to be a U.S. President."

Charles shook his head. "That's ridiculous."

"Is it? One unplayed game of Chinese checkers was all it took to change our life." Chuck shifted uncomfortably on the bed, clearly in pain. "Do you know a man named Albert Ford? Works in accounting?"

Charles was caught off guard by the apparent non sequitur. "I'm sorry, who?"

"Albert Ford. Accounting."

"At . . . Data Tech?"

"Yeah. Blond hair, thinning on top. Average height?"

"I don't really know him. I mean, I think I've seen him around. . . ."

"If you're not careful, Maggie's going to marry him in a few years."

"Albert *Ford*?"

"Yeah."

"And *Maggie*?"

"Yeah."

Charles shot a long hard look at Chuck. "You've got to be kidding."

"Nope. Wait a few years and you'll see. I was invited to the wedding. If you're smart, you won't make the same mistakes I did, and you won't have to live through *that* laughfest. But even if you don't, you *will* have residual memories. They'll be enough to give you nightmares."

Charles started pacing again. "Tell me about residual memories. I've theorized about them, but when I had one—I remembered meeting Maggie at the Data Tech holiday party—it was much clearer than I'd imagined."

"Some are more clear than others. I don't know why."

Charles glanced briefly at Chuck, and the older man's lips twisted into a half smile.

"Yes, I remember rather vividly what you and Maggie did in that closet this afternoon," Chuck said quietly.

Charles closed his eyes. Oh, God. "I'm sorry. I don't know what it is about her, but I couldn't . . . I didn't . . ." He opened his eyes and met Chuck's level gaze. It was almost like looking into a mirror. "She loves *you*," he said. "And as similar as we are, I'm not you."

"Thank God." Chuck's voice rang with heartfelt conviction.

"You don't understand. I have the power to make you disappear. And by making you disappear, I'll end up taking a different path to the future, a path that virtually guarantees that I'll *never* be you. Not even in seven years. I'm not sure I can handle knowing that I'm not quite the man Maggie loves. I don't think I can handle knowing that she'll always be mourning the loss of a person that I'll never quite become."

"You're so wrong," Chuck argued. "If Maggie loves me, then she loves you, too, because every single bit of you is here, inside of me. The rest of me, the part that's *not* you, is poison. And Maggie knows that, she sees it. There's so much I can't give her."

Charles was silent.

"I've known her for seven years," Chuck continued, "and in only a few days you've given her far more than I ever have. You told her about Steve. You told her how you felt. That's all she ever wanted. It's what I couldn't give her, but you've already gotten past that. She fell in love with me because of the danger, because of the excitement. But with you . . . You've cemented her love for us—for *you*. Don't you see?"

Charles sat down on the edge of the bed, suddenly so tired. When had he last slept? "I have the distinct disadvantage of not having known her for the past seven years," he finally said. "I haven't even known her for seven *days*."

"Double memories," Chuck said again. "You're going to live through everything that I did through double memories. You'll catch up in plenty of time."

Charles smiled. "She's incredible."

"You should tell her you love her."

"But I'm not sure I— You know, it's only been a few days. . . . Assuming that I *love* her seems a little bit premature—"

"Don't forget, I was there too," Chuck reminded him. "In the closet? I remember *exactly* what you were thinking. I remember how you felt. You love her almost as much as I do. In time you'll love her even more."

Charles was silent.

"You have to tell her."

He looked at Chuck sharply, suddenly understanding. "You haven't told her, have you? I can't believe it. After seven years you didn't tell her you love her?"

"Even now, I can't bring myself to say it," Chuck admitted quietly.

"I think you could say it," Charles countered. "I just think you *won't*. I think you figure I'll come off looking like the better man if I say it, but you don't."

Chuck made a sorry attempt at a smile. "We always were too smart for our own good, weren't we, kid?" They sat for a moment in silence. Then Chuck shifted again, in pain. "I know you're going to do the right thing. I just wish you'd do it soon. My leg hurts like a bitch."

"What about Stevie?" Even as Charles said the words he could hear an echo of Maggie's voice. *After all this time Stevie's life is still more important to you than your own.* And he knew what he had to do about Stevie. He had to let him go. Because he *didn't* want to end up like Chuck, burned out and battle-worn, hard and cynical. He didn't want to watch Boyd and Maggie die.

Yet his very attempt to save Maggie would guarantee that he didn't become the man she loved.

"Let him rest in peace," Chuck said quietly. "Spend the rest of your life trying to save the kids who *haven't* died."

Charles stood up. "Do you . . . want me to send her in? To say . . . good-bye?"

Chuck shook his head. "No," he said. "Do it right, Charlie, and you and I will never have to say good-bye to Maggie ever again."

THIRTEEN

Maggie sat on the living-room sofa, watching the sky turn pink and orange through the narrow slit in the picture-window draperies.

She heard the soft rumble of voices fade, heard the bedroom door open and close, heard Charles pause as he came into the room.

"It's Thanksgiving," she said, without even turning to face him. "I just realized. It's Thanksgiving morning."

"Happy Thanksgiving." He sounded anything but happy.

"Charlie, I've been wondering. Chuck said he learned survival skills from his Navy friend. What's his name . . ."

"Boyd Rogers?"

"Yeah. He said Boyd taught him all kinds of tricks *after* he developed time travel. After his life was first threatened. So how come you know all that stuff too? Like doubling back on our six?"

Charles sat down across from her in one of Harmon Gregory's easy chairs. He looked totally wiped out.

"I'm sorry," she said. "You need to sleep and—"

He cut her off. "No. I want to talk. I'd *like* to talk . . . if you don't mind."

"Well, I'm right here—dying to listen."

Charles actually managed a smile. "When I was a kid, after I moved to my great-uncle's in New York City—he was a physicist, did I tell you that?"

Maggie shook her head. "No."

"He worked as a professor at NYU. Brilliant man. But strange. He was certainly not prepared to open his home to a seven-year-old. I think he was intending to send me to boarding school. But then he realized that I understood him when he spoke about his work, so he kept me around. In some ways it was an opportunity—I was auditing courses at NYU by the time I was twelve. But in other ways, living in that mausoleum of a house was . . ."

"Lonely?" Maggie supplied.

Charles nodded. "Very much so." He cleared his throat and shifted uncomfortaly in his seat.

He was talking to her. He was actually volunteering information about himself without her having done more than ask a few simple questions. Maggie found herself holding her breath, hoping he would keep talking, wishing there were some way she could make this easier for him.

But only time would ease his discomfort. Only time would make him see that the trust he placed in her was well justified.

She knew the man he'd become if he didn't risk everything and trust her completely. Chuck hadn't taken that risk seven years ago, and this beautiful, precious, newly formed, and so fragile thing that was the seed of their love had been crushed before it could grow. And Chuck had grown colder, harder. Lonelier. And Maggie had ended up married to some fool.

She looked into Charles's eyes, willing him to take the chance and tell her more.

He looked back, and he began to talk. "The house was so silent—I could think for hours on end without interruption. I read all of the books in my uncle's library, and went to the public library for more. My entire life revolved around my research. I knew there was so much I needed to learn if I was going to develop my theories of time travel. I read, I ate, I slept, and—when Jen, my uncle's housekeeper, remembered to send me—I went to school.

"The year I turned ten, I was walking home from school one day, and a gang of high-school kids grabbed me and pulled me into an alley. They had knives and they threatened to use them if I didn't hand over all my money. But I had none. I had nothing of value to anyone but me. I had a picture of Stevie in my wallet, and when they took that, I . . . lost it. I went ballistic and got myself slashed for my trouble. But even that didn't stop me."

Maggie could picture him, ten years old and wire thin, with that burning intensity turning him into a passionate windmill of pounding fists and kicking feet with no regard for his own safety.

"One of the kids pinned me to the ground while the other kids ran off with my wallet—with my picture of my brother. This kid who held me down—Boyd Rogers—was four years older than me, but it was all he could do to hold me there. I don't know, maybe the way I fought won his respect, but he quieted me down by telling me that if I stopped fighting him, he'd go and get my wallet back. He told me we'd trade—he'd give me the wallet if I would tutor him in science and math.

"At first, I couldn't believe it. I thought he was probably making fun of me, but I would have done anything to get that picture back, so I agreed. And when Boyd upheld his part of the bargain, he held me to mine. It turned out he was serious. He wanted a tutor. So I met him at least three times a week after school, in the park. He got a lot of razzing from his friends for hanging out with a ten-year-old from the School of Gifted Geeks, but he didn't give a damn. You see, he had this plan to join the Navy and become a SEAL the way his cousin had done. And his cousin told him that if he wanted to get into the SEAL units, he had to have a strong background in science and technology. And that's what I helped him with.

"I worked with him for four years—right up until the day he enlisted. And he tutored me during that time too. He taught me how to fight, how to survive on the streets of the meanest city in the world. And he made it impossible for me to shut out the rest of the world. He gave me a life outside of that silent house." He paused. "You know, I've never told any of this to anyone before."

Maggie's heart was in her throat. "I know," she said softly.

"Boyd and I stayed tight, even after he joined the Navy. And when he finally got into the SEALs, back when I was finishing up my doctorate, he started taking me out on survival training missions. He's been like a brother."

He paused again.

"Maggie, I don't want to be responsible for his death."

Maggie looked up to find him studying her face. His eyes were impossibly sad.

"Or yours, either," he added softly. "Especially yours."

She knew what Charles was going to say next, and sure enough, as she looked back toward the window, he said it.

"I'm going to do it." His words seemed to hang in the stillness.

Maggie fixed her gaze firmly on the ever-lightening strip of sky as she nodded. "That's good," she said. "That's what Chuck wants." She straightened her back and forced herself to look at Charles. "It's what *I* want too."

He just gazed at her. He looked so tired, so unhappy, she wanted to reach for him, to comfort him. She wanted him to comfort her.

"He loves you, you know," Charles finally said. "He has for years."

Maggie shook her head. "He's only known me for less than a week. The Maggie he's known for years married some creep from accounting."

"Albert Ford." Charles gave her one of Chuck's crooked half smiles.

"Do you know him?"

"Not well—but enough to advise you not to marry him."

"All right," Maggie said. "I won't."

"Good." He smiled again. "Poor Albert. Little does he realize his entire destiny has just been altered."

"Think of the aggravation—and alimony payments—we've just saved him."

"Of course, it's entirely possible you were earning more than he was. Maybe *you're* the one who's saved from making those alimony payments."

Maggie laughed, and the smile Charles gave her was one of his own—full and warm and filled with pleasure.

But it faded too quickly as they sat for a moment in silence.

"Would you mind—" he started, then stopped.

Maggie didn't say a word. She just waited.

"Would you mind very much if I admitted that I'm . . . scared?"

She shook her head. "No. I would be . . . honored . . . that you shared that with me."

"I keep wondering if this is really the right thing to do. It feels so wrong to give up all those years of research and . . . I can't keep from thinking what if there's something I've missed. What if there's some way . . . ? What if we all just disappeared? Chuck and I could develop the Wells Project on our own."

"With what funding?" Maggie asked quietly. "According to Chuck, even Data Tech had to go to outside sources to get the money necessary to build the Runabout."

"Maybe . . . private investors." Charles was reaching for answers now. "I have some connections—"

"And if you used those connections, Ken Goodwin and Wizard-9 would be able to track you down. And then we'd be right back here, right where we started."

Charles sat for a moment in silence. "It's just . . . It's hard for me to quit."

"It's not quitting. It's foreseeing a dead end and choosing a different path."

"I'm not sure what I'm supposed to do. How I'm supposed to . . ."

"Just decide," she said quietly. "Picture yourself taking another route to the future."

"All right," he said, straightening his shoulders, steeling himself. "I'll submit my resignation to Data Tech first thing tomorrow morning. I'll go back to school, finish up my medical degree. Do you think that's really all it's going to take? A simple decision? Because I've done it. I've decided."

It took all of Maggie's willpower not to glance over her shoulder at the still-dark hallway that led to the bedrooms. Was Chuck already gone? Would it happen just like that? One moment he was there, and the next he was gone?

But then there was a bang as the bedroom door was pushed open.

Maggie turned as Charles jumped to his feet, ready to defend her, if necessary.

But it was Chuck who came into the hallway, hopping out to meet them. The movement jarred his injured leg and made lines of pain stand out around his mouth.

"It's happened." He looked from Maggie to Charles. "I can feel it. I feel . . . different. So why the hell am I still here?" he said, then collapsed onto the floor in a crumpled heap.

Maggie reached him first. "Oh, my God, he's burning up!"

He was. As Charles touched Chuck his skin felt hot and dry. Feverish. And his wound had bled clear through his bandage. His jeans were saturated too. "He's lost a lot of blood."

"We've got to get him to a hospital!"

"We've got to figure out what I did wrong."

Chuck roused, groaning, swearing softly. "Maggie! Oh, God, they shot her! Gotta get up—"

"No, you don't."

"I'm here, Chuck. I'm all right. You're just having a nightmare." The sound of Maggie's voice seemed to soothe him and he quieted.

Charles took charge. "Grab his feet," he told Maggie. "Help me get him back into bed."

The sheets were stained a bright shade of red. Charles lowered Chuck down on top of them anyway.

Now what?

Chuck was in a great deal of pain, made worse by his feverish state. He drifted, hovering across the line of consciousness, on the edge of some terrible, nightmarish place, and he fought to stay awake.

"Get a towel," Charles ordered Maggie, and as she vanished back into the hallway he glared down at Chuck. "For a registered genius, you are one hell of an idiot. How could you possibly have forgotten the basic rule of first aid? Apply pressure to stop bleeding."

Chuck was pale, nearly gray looking, and his teeth chattered from a sudden chill. "I did. In the car. It stopped."

"Yeah? It looks like it started again."

"I didn't think I'd be around long enough for it to matter."

"Well, I've made my decision. No way am I following *your* path. But you're still here, so it looks like I'm going to have to do more than simply make up my mind to change my future. I don't suppose you have any suggestions?"

Silently, Maggie appeared, holding the towel out for Charles. He took it, using it to gently apply pressure over the makeshift bandage.

"I'll find some blankets," Maggie murmured, taking one look at the way Chuck was shivering.

"Thanks," Charles said.

She met his eyes briefly before she left the room. Her own gaze was decidedly sober. She knew as well as he did that their situation had just dropped from bad to worse.

Chuck had drifted off again, before offering up any suggestions.

Charles had to answer for him as Maggie brought a pile of blankets into the room and began covering Chuck. "Maybe I have to take action," he suggested, helping her. "Maybe I should call Randy Lowenstein. Tell him right now—today—that I'm leaving Data Tech. I could call John Fairfield at NYU. He always promised that he'd do whatever was necessary to get me into the medical school at the university. He was a friend of my uncle's," he explained to Maggie, "who always wanted me to complete my degree and go into medical research."

He made the phone calls quickly, from the telephone on the bedside table, as he continued to apply pressure to Chuck's still-bleeding leg. He turned slightly away, because he didn't want to see Maggie sit down next to Chuck, on the edge of the bed. But she didn't. Instead, she sat quietly on the floor, away from both of them, leaning back against the wall. She tucked the shortened skirt of her dress in and pulled her knees tightly to her chest, wrapping her arms around them.

He could feel her watching him as he spoke on the phone, and he felt a pang of longing so sharp, he had to clear his throat before he could talk. Chuck loved her enough to die for her. How could he possibly compete with that? After all this was over, what would happen? Would Maggie even want to see him again, or would he remind her too much of Chuck?

And if he asked her, would she come with him to New York? He honestly didn't know. But he wanted her to. He wanted it more than he'd ever wanted anything.

More than he wanted to find a way to travel through time.

He dropped the phone back into the receiver, and Chuck fought to open his eyes. "I'm still here," he whispered.

Randy Lowenstein had expressed regrets about Charles's decision to leave Data Tech, but he'd been supportive and had wished him luck. Dr. John Fairfield, a man whose anatomy classes Charles had audited while still only a child, had been overjoyed that he was intending to complete his medical degree. Fairfield had never understood that Charles had needed to know enough about the human body to make sure that his time-travel device delivered a living, breathing person rather than some compressed bundle of protoplasm to the past. That was Charles's sole purpose for studying medicine. Achieving a medical degree to dangle off the end of his name meant nothing to him. At least not until now.

But despite the sense of forward motion he'd gotten from his phone calls, nothing—apparently—had changed.

"Maybe I need to do more." Charles rubbed his eyes with his free hand, wishing there was time to lie down, to take a nap. He wanted to sit down next to Maggie and pull her into his arms. But he wouldn't do that. Not in front of Chuck. "Maybe I need to erase my hard drive. Maybe I need to delete the files of my research notes."

It would damn near kill him to wipe out nearly three decades' worth of research. But he was going to have to do it—because he didn't want to end up lying on that bed with a bullet in his leg, filled with vividly violent dreams caused by extremely nonresidual memories of Maggie bleeding to death as he held her in his arms.

"Maybe," Maggie said quietly from where she was sitting on the floor, "Chuck hasn't left because Ken Goodwin is still out there somewhere. Maybe this has to do with him. Maybe until we confront him . . ."

Charles turned to look at Chuck. "Confront Goodwin . . . ?"

Chuck didn't answer, held prisoner by his feverish dreams.

And then the doorbell rang.

FOURTEEN

Charles turned toward the living room and froze, a look of intense concentration on his face, as if he were waiting for something, listening—for what?

Maggie's heart was pounding so loudly, it seemed impossible that he could hear anything over it at all.

"Who do you think it is?" she breathed.

He shook his head very slightly, his eyes still unfocused, still listening.

"Charlie, do you think it's . . . ?" Ken Goodwin. She couldn't bring herself to say the name. It was impossible, anyway. How could he have found them here?

Charles unfroze, glancing first at Chuck, who tossed feverishly on the bed, then turning to meet her gaze. She knew what he was thinking. If it *was* Ken Goodwin, he was virtually on his own. Chuck was out for the count.

"I don't think he'd stop to ring the doorbell," he said. But just the same, he held out his hand for hers, hoisting her to her feet. "Help me move Chuck into the closet. I want you in there with him until I know for sure what's—"

On the other side of the room, a window shattered with a crash, the curtain billowing as the figure of a man kicked his way through.

Maggie heard herself scream, a scream that ended abruptly as the weight of Charles's body pushed her down onto the floor and knocked all of the air from her lungs. But then Charles was up again, reaching for Chuck, pulling him off the bed and down, nearly on top of them, as the gunman opened fire.

The noise was deafening in the small bedroom. Again, Charles covered her. The mirror on the wall above them shattered, raining shards of glass down on top of them.

But then the shooting stopped.

"I think that's enough," a voice said. "Don't you?"

Charles shifted slightly, and Maggie could see the leader of Wizard-9, Ken Goodwin, standing in the doorway of the room, holding a gun. From his vantage point, he could easily kill them all. He must've come in through the front door.

He nodded a polite greeting, as if he were paying a social call. "Ms. Winthrop. And the Doctors Della Croce. You didn't honestly think I wouldn't be able to find you?" He smiled. "That bullet the elder Dr. Della Croce has in his leg is part of a little pet project I've been working on over at the Wizard-9 labs. It's specifically designed to lose velocity upon impact and remain embedded in the recipient's body, where it acts as a homing device. Clever, don't you think, Ms. Winthrop?"

Charles moved so he was directly in front of Maggie.

His face was bleeding. He'd been cut by the flying glass just below his left eye. He wiped the blood away as if it were merely an inconvenience. "You keep that gun aimed away from her."

"Take care of those weapons," Goodwin said to his hired gun, motioning with his head toward Chuck's assault weapon hanging on the bedpost and the handgun on the bedside table.

Charles pulled himself to his feet, carefully keeping Maggie behind him as the gunman followed orders. Chuck still lay on the floor, caught in a feverish nightmare. Charles's own nightmare was far too real.

He could feel Maggie's fingers wrapped tightly around his arm.

"Step away from her, Doctor," Goodwin said almost gently.

"I don't think so." Charles inched his hand down toward the pocket of his jacket. Chuck had been right. If he had to, he would use whatever means possible to protect Maggie.

Maggie's voice was low and urgent. "Charlie, whatever happens, whatever he does, don't continue with the Wells Project. It's not worth it—*I'm* not worth it. I know you don't love me, you couldn't possibly—you don't even really know me and—"

"Move away from her, Della Croce," Goodwin said again as Charles slipped his fingers beneath the edge of his pocket. "You're an extremely intelligent man. No doubt you've figured out what I have to do to guarantee your continued participation in this project."

"Just keep thinking about New York," Maggie told him fiercely. "If you give in and do what he says, he'll use you for as long as he needs you and then he'll kill you anyway. If I'm going to die, at least let my death *mean* something." Her voice shook. "Promise me, Charlie. Let me at least hold on to those pictures of you in New York. I have to believe you'll get there—that you'll be all right."

How could she think that? How could she imagine he'd be all right anywhere without her? But then Charles knew. He'd never told her he loved her. And he did. He loved her.

"Put this one up on the bed." Goodwin nudged Chuck with his foot as he spoke to his gunman. "And rouse him. I want him to be awake."

This was it. Charles knew this was his chance. As the gunman slipped his own weapon over his shoulder and bent down to lift Chuck onto the bed, Charles dropped his hand into his jacket pocket, praying the handgun Chuck had given him hours before was pointing in the right direction.

It was.

He aimed it at Goodwin and fired, right through his pocket, like some kind of dime-novel gangster.

It all happened so fast. The look of shock on Goodwin's face. The bloom of bright red on the white of his shirt. Maggie's hands pushing him away, pushing him down. The sound of Goodwin's gun as he squeezed off one final shot before his knees crumpled and he sank lifelessly to the ground.

And just like that, Goodwin vanished.

The gunman staggered back with a cry of alarm as Charles scrambled to his knees, pulling his gun free from his pocket. As he aimed the handgun at the man he saw from the corner of his eye that Chuck, too, had disappeared.

"I have no desire to kill you too," he told the gunman. "Just slowly put down your weapons."

The man's hands were shaking as he obeyed.

"The girl's been hit," he said.

The words didn't make any sense to Charles. At least not at first. The girl's been . . . ?

But then he turned and saw the blood.

Maggie.

Charles dropped his gun, fear and anguish hitting him like a battering ram to the chest. Goodwin's final bullet had hit Maggie.

"Call 9-1-1," he shouted as he reached for her, searching for her pulse, praying she was still alive. But the gunman was already gone, out of the room, the front door slamming behind him.

The bullet had gone in her lower back, just below the ribs, as she'd pushed him down and thrown herself across him. Once again, she'd taken the shot that was meant to kill him.

He reached for the phone himself, dialing the emergency number as he worked desperately to stop her bleeding.

"Don't die," he told her. "Goddammit, I'm not going to let you die!"

❖━━━━━━━❖

"Dr. Della Croce?"

Charles looked up warily as the police detective came into the small cinder-block room.

He'd been questioned for hours, first at the hospital, and then here, in this interrogation room at the police station. He'd told his story over and over again to all shapes and sizes of detectives. To the precinct captain. To a psychiatrist who was clearly trying to evaluate his sanity.

He knew it sounded crazy. Time travel. Who would possibly believe it?

The worst of it was, they seemed to think he was the one who had shot Maggie.

Maggie's surgery had taken an interminable amount of time. She'd come through it alive, but when he'd been taken from the hospital she still wasn't out of danger. She was placed under guard in the intensive-care unit.

Charles wanted to be there, sitting next to her, holding her hand, telling her to hang on, to fight to stay alive.

Telling her that he loved her.

Instead, he'd been taken here. And while he hadn't quite been put in a jail cell, the door to this little room had been securely locked each time he'd been left alone.

He'd tried to focus his thoughts on Maggie, tried to reach out to her across all the city blocks that separated them.

Her love for him had defied the boundaries of time. Surely his could touch her across such a short physical distance. . . .

"How is she?" he asked the detective, praying that the news was good.

"She's corroborated your story," the man told him.

Charles's heart leaped and he stood up. "She's conscious?"

"Yeah. Not that we believe her any more than we believe you, but at least we seem to have removed you from our list of suspects. Ms. Winthrop insists you didn't shoot her. Although I think it's the fact that the ballistics lab verified that the bullet the doctors took out of her didn't come from your gun that's working the most in your favor."

"I want to see her."

"Well, she's asking for you, too," the detective told him. "So let's go."

The drive to the hospital took forever, as did the elevator up to the intensive-care unit, but finally Charles was there.

Maggie was asleep. She looked so tiny in that bed, hooked up to every monitor imaginable. An IV tube was attached to a bag that sent a slow but steady drip of a powerful painkiller into her arm. Charles took her chart from the foot of her bed.

"You can't read that," the nurse admonished him.

He gave her a long, level look. "Yes," he said. "I can."

She was silent as he opened Maggie's chart and quickly read the doctor's notes, saw from where the bullet had been removed, saw that it hadn't come near her spine, saw that none of the damage it had done would be permanent.

Her injuries were serious, but she would live.

If she wanted to.

The nurse watched him warily as he replaced the chart.

"I'm going to sit with her," he told the woman.

"Visitors aren't supposed to stay long," she told him. "There's no chair."

"Then I'll stand." Charles reached out gently and touched Maggie's hair, touched her hand. "Hey, Maggie," he said quietly, unable to keep his eyes from filling with tears. "I'm here." His voice broke and he couldn't go on. All he could do was hold her hand, hope that she felt the pressure of his fingers against hers. He didn't care what anyone said, he wasn't leaving her side again. He needed her to hang on. He needed her to come back to him. He wanted her to open her eyes and look at him while he told her that he loved her.

The nurse stood and watched him for several long minutes before she silently left the room.

She came back with a chair.

Charles couldn't remember the last time he'd slept. But every time he felt himself start to drift off, he forced himself to sit up straighter and have another cup of coffee.

He was determined to keep talking to Maggie. He was sure that somewhere, even if only in the back of her subconscious mind, she could hear him.

And he wanted to make sure he was there and awake when she opened her eyes again.

At first the nurses tried to talk him into taking a nap. But after a while they gave up and brought him a fresh cup of coffee every time they came in to check on Maggie.

The only problem with coffee was that after drinking about three cups, he was forced to leave Maggie's side for a minute or two.

And naturally, he was in the bathroom when she woke up.

"She's asking for you," one of the nurses told him as he walked out of the men's room.

Charles ran down the hall, praying that he'd get to her before she slipped back into a painkiller-induced sleep.

He burst through the door. "Maggie!"

Her eyes were closed, but she spoke. "Chuck."

Chuck. She wanted Chuck.

Charles felt sick. He felt his heart drop down into his stomach. She wanted Chuck, but Chuck was gone. Forever.

He felt a surge of emotions. Grief for her loss. The pain and despair of his own dashed hopes and expectations. Fear that if she knew the truth, if she knew Chuck was gone, she'd give up her fight to stay alive.

Charles reached for her hand, uncertain how to tell her.

As his fingers touched hers her eyes opened.

He could see both her pain and the medication she was being given to numb it in her eyes. She was barely able to focus, and she blinked up at him, trying to clear her foggy vision.

"Chuck," she said again.

The cut on his cheek. No doubt she saw it and in her

grogginess she mistook him for his future self. He started to shake his head, to tell her no, but she reached for him, pulling him closer, clearly wanting to tell him something of great importance.

"Chuck, it's . . . okay," she breathed. "You can go now. I'm going to be all right."

She tried to squeeze his hand, but her grip was impossibly weak. Charles couldn't speak. He didn't know what to say.

"I love you," she whispered. "I'll always love you, and remember you. But I have to . . . be honest."

She fell into a silence that lasted so long, Charles pulled back slightly, thinking she was once again asleep. But her eyes were still open. They were filled with tears.

"I know why you wanted me and Charlie . . . to be together. You were right. . . ."

"I don't understand. . . ."

"You knew if I could love you, if I could love the man you've become, despite all you've done and all you wouldn't tell me . . . then I would love Charlie even more." Her eyes closed and the last of her words were spoken on a sigh. "And I do."

Charles sent a silent prayer of thanks to Chuck, wherever he was. It didn't matter that he wasn't going to take Chuck's dark and dangerous path. It didn't matter that he was never going to become Chuck.

He was already something better than Chuck.

He was Charlie.

And Maggie loved him, just the way he was.

Maggie's throat was sore. Her mouth and tongue were dry and tasted like the floor of a barn.

Her eyelids were heavy and glued shut. It took close to forever to pry them open, but when she did, she was rewarded by the sight of Charles, fast asleep in a chair next to her bed.

From the looks of the hospital room, from the number of empty coffee cups scattered around the room, he appeared to have moved in.

How long had she been here?

Judging from the growth of stubble on Charles's chin, it had been quite a few days.

She tried to moisten her lips to speak, but when she opened her mouth, she made barely more than a dry-sounding rattle.

Nevertheless, Charles sat up, instantly alert.

"Hey," he said, his lips curving up into one of his truly fabulous smiles.

He poured some water from a pitcher into a waiting cup, and held it out for her, positioning the straw so that it reached her lips.

The water was almost as refreshing as his smile, and she sighed deeply with contentment—then realized that deep sighs, in fact, deep breaths of any kind, were no longer in her repertoire.

"Hurts, huh?" Charles's eyes were dark with concern as she stifled a groan.

"Yeah," she managed to rasp.

"You're going to be okay." He took her hand. "You woke up just in time to watch them move you out of the ICU."

The cut on his cheek was starting to heal. "You're

going to have a scar," Maggie whispered, "right where Chuck did."

Charles nodded. "Probably."

"Funny," she said.

"He's gone, you know."

Maggie looked into Charles's eyes. "Not all of him. Not the best part of him."

He gave another of those slow, wonderful smiles. "We've been driving the police crazy, you and I."

She laughed, and discovered that laughing was something else she shouldn't do a great deal of for a while.

"I told them the truth," he continued after she'd recovered slightly, "but they haven't exactly taken the time-travel part of the story and embraced it. They remain stumped by the blood on the sheets. They've done DNA testing, and it's obviously my blood, but they know that amount couldn't possibly have come from the cut on my cheek. . . . I told them about Chuck being shot, but every time I mention him, they send another shrink in to evaluate me.

"And the bullet they took out of you—it's unlike anything they've ever seen before. But whenever I tell them it came from a gun that was made seven years in the future, they get really tense."

Maggie bit her lip. "Don't make me laugh!"

"Enough of the neighbors saw Goodwin's hired gun running out of the house. I think the police suspect we were being held hostage by him, and that the trauma created this odd delusion we share about time travelers."

"I don't care what they think," Maggie told him. "I'm just glad that it's over."

Charles nodded. His eyes were soft as he touched her hair, as his thumb stroked her cheek.

"So," she said a bit breathlessly, "you're off to New York."

Something shifted in his eyes. "I am."

Silence. Maggie broke it by clearing her throat. "So," she said again. "I guess I'm wondering if you're going to ask me to come along, or if you're going to let me slip away. What's it gonna be, Charlie? Are you going to spend the next seven years pining away for me the way you did the first time around?"

Her words didn't get the smile she expected. In fact, he took them dead seriously, not as the rather lame joke she'd intended.

"I think," he said slowly, "I'm the only man in the world who can learn from mistakes that I haven't even made yet." He paused, and Maggie nearly drowned in the midnight darkness of his eyes. "Maggie, please do me the honor of becoming my wife and come to New York with me."

Maggie laughed, then grimaced in pain. Of all the things she'd suspected he'd say, *that* wasn't one of them. Marry her. He wanted to *marry* her. Was it possible . . . ?

Maggie searched his eyes and found what she was looking for. *Yes.* He loved her. It wasn't like Chuck's love—fueled by years of disappointment and frustration and pain. Instead it was new and fresh, like her own love for him, accompanied by wonder and delight and that ever-burning heat of desire. Her eyes filled with tears. "Oh, Charlie—"

He leaned over and kissed her gently.

"I love you, Maggie," he told her, almost as an after-thought. "You have no idea how much."

Maggie smiled. "Yes, I do. And yes, I'll marry you." She knew that he loved her just from looking into his eyes.

But she sure did like to hear the words.

EPILOGUE

He stood in the bedroom, dizzy, wondering what he was doing there. He'd come upstairs to get something and then . . .

The room seemed somehow different to him. The carpeting softer, the colors more subdued, the floral-patterned bedspread unfamiliar. And the view out the window . . .

It wasn't the desert. Instead of the flat arid landscape, he found himself looking out at snow-covered hills. New England, he remembered suddenly. This wasn't Arizona. It was Massachusetts.

It was Thanksgiving in Massachusetts. It was their third Thanksgiving in this house in this little town that he and Maggie loved so much.

Maggie . . .

He turned as he heard her push open the door, as she came into the bedroom. *Their* bedroom.

She was wearing a dark blue velvet dress that swept

all the way to the ground and almost entirely concealed her softly swelling abdomen. Their second baby. She was pregnant with their second child. She wore her hair down around her shoulders, and as she gazed at him she looked so beautiful, his breath caught in his throat.

His wife. Of nearly seven years now.

"Are you okay?" she asked softly.

He nodded, unable to speak. He couldn't remember the last time he'd been this happy. Yet, at the same time, he *could* remember. He could remember every single day of the past seven years, waking up with Maggie in his bed. He remembered the joy of shared mornings and the quiet intimacy of late nights spent talking and making love.

He remembered the afternoon nearly three years earlier when he'd helped his wife give birth to their daughter, Annie. He remembered holding their precious baby in his arms, of rocking her to sleep. He remembered the chubby toddler Annie had become, the way she raced to greet him every day when he came home from work. He remembered it all. It was so good, so sweet. It was the life he'd always dreamed of having.

He could tell from the way Maggie was standing, from the look in her eyes, that she knew. She stepped forward unhesitatingly, into his embrace, and he held her tightly, so much so that he was afraid he might hurt her. But she held him just as close.

"Hello, Chuck," she whispered.

"Mags." It was all he could manage to say before he kissed her.

It was funny. The pain in his leg. The fever from the bullet wound. Gone. All gone. All of the anger and resentiment and bitterness he'd carried with him for so long was gone. Just like that. Gone. He'd thought he'd simply be gone as well, but he'd been wrong. . . .

He wasn't gone. He was back in his own time. But it was a different time. A better time.

And he was Chuck, but . . . he wasn't. He felt so different. So happy. So at peace and so content with his life.

He'd thought that wanting Maggie so desperately for seven years, that loving her from a distance, had made his love so powerful, so sharp and strong.

But he realized now that the love he felt in those rapidly fading memories was nothing compared with the incredible love that had grown from having and holding her for the past seven years.

He didn't want to be Chuck. And he wasn't. Not anymore. Not ever again.

She pulled back to gaze into his eyes, and it was as if she could read his mind. She gave him one of her wonderful, gorgeous smiles. "You're Charlie now."

He managed to smile, too, despite the tears in his eyes. "I am. Thank God." And he was. The memories he had of the past seven years of his life with Maggie were so much stronger, so much more real than the ghostly echo of that other life he'd had.

Maggie stood on her toes to kiss him again, and Charlie felt himself sigh.

He was Charlie Della Croce, and he was home.

THE EDITORS' CORNER

As the year draws to a close, we're delighted to bring you some Christmas cheer to warm and gladden your hearts. December's LOVESWEPTs will put a smile on your face and love on your mind, and when you turn that last page, you'll sigh longingly and maybe even wipe a few stray tears off your cheeks.

Rachel Lawrence and Sam Wyatt are setting off **FIREWORKS** in LOVESWEPT #862 by rising star RaeAnne Thayne. The last time Rachel left Whiskey Creek, she swore she'd never return. The only two people in the world who can force her to break her vow are her nephews. The problem is, Rachel and their father, Sam, can't stand each other. Now that Rachel's back in town, the sparks are flying. Sam can't understand why Rachel would take such a vested interest in the welfare of his sons—he just wants her to leave before he acts on the desire he feels for her. Rachel fears giving in to feelings for Sam she's harbored in her heart, harbored even before she lost her young husband in a brushfire. But when another brushfire threatens to claim the family ranch, will she forgive Sam for choosing duty over love? RaeAnne Thayne's tale sizzles with passion and is sure to keep you warm on even the coldest winter night!

In LOVESWEPT #863, Laura Taylor delivers **THE CHRISTMAS GIFT.** Former attorney Jack Howell thought his toughest cases were behind him, but when he returns to Kentucky to explore his new-found roots, he faces his most baffling case of all—an infant boy abandoned on his doorstep. Interior decorator Chloe McNeil's temper starts to simmer when Jack doesn't keep their appointment to discuss his new home. Maybe she's misjudged this man who so easily found a way into her heart. But when she drops by to give him a piece of her mind, she finds him knee-deep in diapers and formula. As Jack and Chloe care for the baby and try to keep Social Services from taking him away, will they discover that cherishing this child together is just the healing magic they need? Well-loved author Laura Taylor unites two wounded spirits during the season of Christmas harmony.

Remember Candy Johnson, Jen Casey's best friend in FOR LOVE OR MONEY, LOVESWEPT #849? Well, she's back with a hunk of her own in Kathy DiSanto's **HUNTER IN DISGUISE,** LOVE-SWEPT #864. Candy is sure there's more to George Price than his chunky glasses and ever-present pocket protector. For example, a chest and tush of Greek-god standards. And why would a gym teacher take out the soccer balls for the girls vs. guys volleyball match? And let's not forget about his penchant for B 'n' E (breaking and entering, that is). In the meantime, George has a problem all his own—trying to distract armchair detective Candy long enough to get his job done. George's less-than-debonair attributes prove to be easy enough to ignore as Candy gets to know the man beneath the look. Kathy DiSanto spins a breathless tale that's part wicked romp, part sexy suspense, and all pure pleasure!

Please welcome newcomer Catherine Mulvany to our Loveswept family as she presents **UPON A MIDNIGHT CLEAR**, LOVESWEPT #865. Alexandra Roundtree's obituary clearly stated she was no longer one of Brunswick, Oregon's, living citizens, but private investigator Dixon Yano is disabused of that notion when she comes walking into his agency in full disguise. Alex pleads with Dixon to help her find her would-be murderer, and after shots are fired through his window, Dixon decides to be her bodyguard. Soon, Dixon and Alex are forced into close quarters and intimate encounters. Even after her last romantic fiasco, Alex finds herself trusting in the man who has become her swashbuckling hero and lifesaver. Will Dixon cross the line between business and pleasure if it means risking his lady's life? Catherine Mulvany's first novel mixes up an explosively sensual cocktail that will touch and tantalize the soul!

Happy reading!

With warmest wishes,

Susann Brailey

Joy Abella

Susann Brailey
Senior Editor

Joy Abella
Administrative Editor

P.S. Look for these Bantam women's fiction titles coming in December! *New York Times* bestseller Iris Johansen is back with **LONG AFTER MIDNIGHT,** now available in paperback. Research scientist Kate Denham mistakenly believes she's finally carved out a secure life for herself and her son, only to be thrown suddenly into a nightmare world where danger is all around and trusting a handsome stranger is the only way to survive. Hailed as "a queen of erotic, exciting romance," Susan Johnson gives us **TABOO.** Andre Duras and Teo Korsakova are thrown together during the chaotic times of the Napoleonic Wars, igniting a glorious passion even as conflicting loyalties threaten to tear them apart. And finally, a charmer from the gifted Michelle Martin—**STOLEN MOMENTS**—a stylish contemporary romance about the man hired to track down a beautiful young pop singer who is tired of fame and has decided to explore Manhattan incognito. And immediately following this page, preview the Bantam women's fiction titles on sale in October!

For current information on Bantam's women's fiction, visit our Web site, *Isn't It Romantic,* at the following address: **http://www.bdd.com/romance**

Don't miss these extraordinary books
by your favorite Bantam authors!

On sale in October:

FINDING LAURA
by Kay Hooper

HAWK O'TOOLE'S HOSTAGE
by Sandra Brown

IT HAPPENED ONE NIGHT
by Leslie LaFoy

POWER AND MONEY ARE NO PROTECTION FROM FATE— OR MURDER. . . .

FINDING LAURA
by Kay Hooper

Over the years, the wealthy, aloof Kilbourne family has suffered a number of suspicious deaths. Now the charming, seductive Peter Kilbourne has been found stabbed to death in a seedy motel room. And for Laura Sutherland, a struggling artist, nothing will ever be the same. Because she was one of the last people to see him alive—and one of the first to be suspected of his murder.

Now, determined to clear her name and uncover the truth about the murder—and the antique mirror that had recently brought Peter into her life—Laura will breach the iron gates of the Kilbourne estate . . . only to find that every Kilbourne, from the enigmatic Daniel to the steely matriarch Amelia to Peter's disfigured widow, Kerry, has something to hide. But which one of them looks in the mirror and sees the reflection of a killer? And which one will choose Laura to be the next to die?

"Miss Sutherland? I'm Peter Kilbourne."

A voice to break hearts.

Laura gathered her wits and stepped back, opening the door wider to admit him. "Come in." She thought he was about her own age, maybe a year or two older.

He came into the apartment and into the living room, taking in his surroundings quickly but thoroughly, and clearly taking note of the mirror on the coffee table. His gaze might have widened a bit when it fell on her collection of mirrors, but Laura couldn't be sure, and when he turned to face her, he was smiling with every ounce of his charm.

It was unsettling how instantly and powerfully she was affected by that magnetism. Laura had never considered herself vulnerable to charming men, but she knew without doubt that this one would be difficult to resist—whatever it was he wanted of her. Too uneasy to sit down or invite him to, Laura merely stood with one hand on the back of a chair and eyed him with what she hoped was a faint, polite smile.

If Peter Kilbourne thought she was being ungracious in not inviting him to sit down, he didn't show it. He gestured slightly toward the coffee table and said, "I see you've been hard at work, Miss Sutherland."

She managed a shrug. "It was badly tarnished. I wanted to get a better look at the pattern."

He nodded, his gaze tracking past her briefly to once again note the collection of mirrors near the hallway. "You have quite a collection. Have you . . . always collected mirrors?"

It struck her as an odd question somehow, perhaps because there was something hesitant in his tone, something a bit surprised in his eyes. But Laura replied truthfully despite another stab of uneasiness. "Since I was a child, actually. So you can see why I bought that one today at the auction."

"Yes." He slid his hands into the pockets of his dark slacks, sweeping open his suit jacket as he did so in a pose that might have been studied or merely relaxed. "Miss Sutherland—look, do you mind if I call you Laura?"

"No, of course not."

"Thank you," he nodded gravely, a faint glint of amusement in his eyes recognizing her reluctance. "I'm Peter."

She nodded in turn, but didn't speak.

"Laura, would you be interested in selling the mirror back to me? At a profit, naturally."

"I'm sorry." She was shaking her head even before he finished speaking. "I don't want to sell the mirror."

"I'll give you a hundred for it."

Laura blinked in surprise, but again shook her head. "I'm not interested in making money, Mr. Kilbourne—"

"Peter."

A little impatiently, she said, "All right—Peter. I don't want to sell the mirror. And I did buy it legitimately."

"No one's saying you didn't, Laura," he soothed. "And you aren't to blame for my mistake, certainly. Look, the truth is that the mirror shouldn't have been put up for auction. It's been in my family a long time, and we'd like to have it back. Five hundred."

Not a bad profit on a five-dollar purchase. She drew a breath and spoke slowly. "No. I'm sorry, I really am, but . . . I've been looking for this—for a mirror like this—for a long time. To add to my collection. I'm not interested in making money, so please don't bother to raise your offer. Even five thousand wouldn't make a difference."

His eyes were narrowed slightly, very intent on her face, and when he smiled suddenly it was with rueful certainty. "Yes, I can see that. You don't have to look so uneasy, Laura—I'm not going to wrest the thing away from you by force."

"I never thought you would," she murmured, lying.

He chuckled, a rich sound that stroked along her nerve endings like a caress. "No? I'm afraid I've made you nervous, and that was never my intention. Why don't I buy you dinner some night as an apology?"

This man is dangerous. "That isn't necessary," she said.

"I insist."

Laura looked at his incredibly handsome face, that charming smile, and drew yet another deep breath. "Will your wife be coming along?" she asked mildly.

"If she's in town, certainly." His eyes were guileless.

Very dangerous. Laura shook her head. "Thanks, but no apology is necessary. You offered a generous price for the mirror; I refused. That's all there is to it." She half turned and made a little gesture toward the door with one hand, unmistakably inviting him to leave.

Peter's beautiful mouth twisted a bit, but he obeyed the gesture and followed her to the door. When she opened it and stood back, he paused to reach into the inner pocket of his jacket and produced a business card. "Call me if you change your mind," he said. "About the mirror, I mean."

Or anything else, his smile said.

"I'll do that," she returned politely, accepting the card.

"It was nice meeting you, Laura."

"Thank you. Nice meeting you," she murmured.

He gave her a last flashing smile, lifted a hand slightly in a small salute, and left her apartment.

Laura closed the door and leaned back against it for a moment, relieved and yet still uneasy. She didn't know why Peter Kilbourne wanted the mirror back badly enough to pay hundreds of dollars for it, but every instinct told her the matter was far from settled.

She hadn't heard the last of him.

Her novels are sensual and moving, compelling and richly satisfying. That's why *New York Times* bestselling phenomenon **Sandra Brown** is one of America's best-loved romance writers. Now, the passionate struggle between a modern-day outlaw and his feisty, beautiful captive erupts in

HAWK O'TOOLE'S HOSTAGE

To Hawk O'Toole, she was a pawn in a desperate gamble to help his people. To Miranda Price, he was a stranger who'd done the unthinkable: kidnapped her and her young son off a train full of sight-seeing vacationers. Now, held hostage on a distant reservation for reasons she cannot at first fathom, Miranda finds herself battling a captor who is by turns harsh and tender, mysteriously aloof and dangerously seductive.

"You know me?" She tried not to reveal her anxiety through her voice.

"I know who you are."

"Then you have me at a distinct disadvantage."

"That's right. I do."

She had hoped to weasel out his name, but he lapsed into stoic silence as the horse carefully picked its way down the steep incline. As hazardous as the race up the mountainside had been, traveling down the other side was more so. Miranda expected the horse's forelegs to buckle at any second and pitch them forward. They wouldn't stop rolling until they hit bottom several miles below. She was afraid for

Scott. He was still crying, though not hysterically as before.

"That man my son is riding with, does he know how to ride well?"

"Ernie was practically born on a horse. He won't let anything happen to the boy. He's got several sons of his own."

"Then he must understand how I feel!" she cried.

When she reflexively laid her hand on his thigh, she inadvertently touched his holster. The pistol was within her grasp! All she had to do was play it cool. If she could catch him off guard, she had a chance of whipping the pistol out of the holster and turning it on him. She could stave off the others while holding their leader at gunpoint long enough for Scott to get on the horse with her. Surely she could find her way back to the train where law enforcement agencies must already be organizing search parties. Their trail wouldn't be difficult to follow, for no efforts had been taken to cover it. They could still be found well before dark.

But in the meantime, she had to convince the outlaw that she was resigned to her plight and acquiescent to his will. Gradually, so as not to appear obvious, she let her body become more pliant against his chest. She ceased trying to maintain space between her thighs and his. She no longer kept her hip muscles contracted, but let them go soft against his lap, which grew perceptibly tighter and harder with each rocking motion of the saddle.

Eventually her head dropped backward onto his shoulder, as though she had dozed off. She made certain he could see that her eyes were closed. She knew he was looking down at her because she could feel his breath on her face and the side of her neck. Taking a deep breath, she intentionally lifted her breasts high, until they strained against her lightweight summer blouse. When they settled, they settled heavily on the arm he still held across her midriff.

But she didn't dare move her hand, not until she thought the moment was right. By then her heart had begun to pound so hard she was afraid he might feel it against his arm. Sweat had moistened her palms. She hoped her hand wouldn't be too slippery to grab the butt of the pistol. To avoid that, she knew she must act without further delay.

In one motion, she sat up straight and reached for the pistol.

He reacted quicker.

His fingers closed around her wrist like a vise and prized her hand off the gun. She grunted in pain and gave an anguished cry of defeat and frustration.

"Mommy?" Scott shouted from up ahead. "Mommy, what's the matter?"

Her teeth were clenched against the pain the outlaw was inflicting on the fragile bones of her wrist, but she managed to choke out, "Nothing, darling. Nothing. I'm fine." Her captor's grip relaxed, and she called to Scott, "How are you?"

"I'm thirsty and I have to go to the bathroom."

"Tell him it's not much farther."

She repeated the dictated message to her son. For the time being Scott seemed satisfied. Her captor let the others go on ahead until the last horse was almost out of sight before he placed one hand beneath her jaw and jerked her head around to face him.

"If you want to handle something hard and deadly, Mrs. Price, I'll be glad to direct your hand to something just as steely and fully loaded as the pistol. But then you already know how hard it is, don't you?

You've been grinding your soft little tush against it for the last twenty minutes." His eyes darkened. "Don't underestimate me again."

The situation had taken on a surreal aspect.

That was dispelled the moment the man dismounted and pulled her down to stand beside him. After the lengthy horseback ride, her thighs quivered under the effort of supporting her. Her feet were numb. Before she regained feeling in them, Scott hurled his small body at her shins and closed his arms around her thighs, burying his face in her lap.

She dropped to her knees in front of him and embraced him tightly, letting tears of relief roll down her cheeks. They had come this far and had escaped serious injury. She was grateful for that much. After a lengthy bear hug, she held Scott away from her and examined him. He seemed none the worse for wear, except for his eyes, which were red and puffy from crying. She drew him to her chest again and hugged him hard.

Too soon, a long shadow fell across them. Miranda looked up. Their kidnapper had taken off the white duster, his gloves, his gun belt, and his hat. His straight hair was as inky black as the darkness surrounding them. The firelight cast wavering shadows across his face that blunted its sharp angles but made it appear more sinister.

That didn't deter Scott. Before Miranda realized what he was going to do, the child flung himself against the man. He kicked at the long shins with his tennis shoes and pounded the hard, lean thighs with his grubby fists.

"You hurt my mommy. I'm gonna beat you up. You're a bad man. I hate you. I'm gonna kill you. You leave my mommy alone."

His high, piping voice filled the still night air. Miranda reached out to pull Scott back, but the man held up his hand to forestall her. He endured Scott's ineffectual attack until the child's strength had been spent and the boy collapsed into another torrent of tears.

The man took the boy's shoulders between his hands. "You are very brave."

His low, resonant voice calmed Scott instantly. With solemn, tear-flooded eyes, Scott gazed up at the man. "Huh?"

"You are very brave to go up against an enemy so much stronger than yourself." The others in the outlaw band had clustered around them, but the boy had the man's attention. He squatted down, putting himself on eye level with Scott. "It's also a fine thing for a man to defend his mother the way you just did." From a scabbard attached to his belt, he withdrew a knife. Its blade was short, but sufficient. Miranda drew in a quick breath. The man tossed the knife into the air. It turned end over end until he deftly caught it by the tip of the blade. He extended the ivory handle toward Scott.

"Keep this with you. If I ever hurt your mother, you can stab me in the heart with it."

Wearing a serious expression, Scott took the knife. Ordinarily, accepting a gift from a stranger would have warranted parental permission. Scott, his eyes fixed on the man before him, didn't even glance at Miranda. For the second time that afternoon, her son had obeyed this man without consulting her first. That, almost as much as their perilous situation, bothered her.

"Hmm. Can I go to the bathroom now?"

"There is no bathroom here. The best we can offer is the woods."

"That's okay. Sometimes Mommy lets me go outside if we're on picnics and stuff." He sounded agreeable enough, but he glanced warily at the wall of darkness beyond the glow of the campfire.

"Ernie will go with you," Hawk reassured him, pressing his shoulder as he stood up. "When you come back, he'll get you something to drink."

"Okay. I'm kinda hungry, too."

Ernie stepped forward and extended his hand to the boy, who took it without hesitation. They turned and, with the other men, headed toward the campfire. Miranda made to follow. The man named Hawk stepped in front of her and barred her path. "Where do you think you're going?"

"To keep an eye on my son."

"Your son will be fine without you."

"Get out of my way."

Instead, he clasped her upper arms and walked her backward until she came up against the rough bark of a pine tree. Hawk kept moving forward until his body was pinning hers against the tree trunk. The brilliant blue eyes moved over her face, down her neck, and across her chest.

"Your son seems to think you're worth fighting for." His head lowered, coming closer to hers. "Are you?"

"A thrilling romantic adventure woven
with the sparkling combination of magic,
humor, and action."
—Nora Roberts

IT HAPPENED
ONE NIGHT
by Leslie LaFoy

*Alanna Chapman knows that no accountant worth her salt
would leave town during tax season, but now she has no
choice. To honor her aunt's final wishes, the Colorado CPA
has come to the mist-shrouded shores of Ireland, intending
to stay just long enough to accomplish her mission. But on
the mysterious grounds of Carraig Cor, something extraordinary happens: Alanna finds herself catapulted back to the
year 1803. Taken for a "seer" who can foretell Ireland's
future, she becomes the prisoner of a ruthless privateer . . . a dangerously attractive sea captain who has no
doubt that he can bend this modern temptress to his will, to
use her magic powers for his own ends. But when Alanna
crossed over to the nineteenth century, she didn't leave her
independent spirit behind. Now she's looking for a way to
escape the captain's irresistible embrace—and his enemy's
notice—before this perilous adventure costs her her
heart . . . and her life.*

Alanna raced to the door of the cabin, fighting back
panic and daring not a single look back. She knew
with absolute certainty that it wouldn't be long before
he staggered to his feet and came after her, that the
seconds between now and his vengeance were pre-

cious. The latch lifted and the door opened without resistance. Barefoot, with her hair streaming behind her, she fled down a dimly lit corridor toward a short flight of steep stairs. Hiking the gown above her knees, she clambered up the worn wooden steps, taking them two at a time. Her breath ragged and her heart pounding, she burst from the bowels of the ship onto the deck. Sliding to a sudden halt, Alanna glanced about the now clouded night, quickly noting the silent activity of shadowed male shapes and the world which lay beyond her floating prison. No light, of either man or heaven, sought to break the darkness. Her sight adjusted as she gazed to her left and out across the open sea. Turning to her right, she saw, beyond a wide expanse of green water, the rocky shoreline she had glimpsed from the window of Kiervan's cabin.

Ahead of her the ship narrowed to a long thick pole that stretched out over the sea. Alanna whirled about. The doorway from which she had emerged onto the deck sat in the center of a squat, flat-topped blockhouse. A few feet to her left another steep but short flight of stairs led upward. With relief, she noted that the structure didn't fill the entire width of the ship. On both sides, between it and the railings, a wide space permitted easy passage to the rear of the vessel. Pivoting to her right, Alanna dashed for the corner.

She was three-quarters of the way down the deck, with the unmistakable silhouette of a dinghy in sight, when a human shape stepped from around the corner and squarely into her path.

She stumbled to a halt. "Colleen, 'tis dangerous for ye to be topside, don't ye know? Where be Kiervan?"

Paddy. And he showed not the slightest signs of being inebriated. With a sigh of relief, Alanna moved toward him, keeping her voice low as she said, "He's a madman, Mr. O'Connell. He thinks it's 1803. He thinks he's some gun-running privateer."

"But for the first, 'tis all true, colleen. The lad's mind be far sounder than that of most men."

She froze and then managed to sputter, "It's 1997!"

He shook his head. " 'Twas before you climbed the Carraig Cor, to be sure. Least 'twas that time from which Maude promised to return to Erin. Now come along, colleen," he said, stepping forward and extending his hand, "an' I'll be a-seein' ye safely returned to Kiervan's cabin."

She stared at him, shaking her head and backing beyond his reach. "You're just as crazy as he is."

" 'Tis a long day ye've had, to be sure, an' 'twill be only a long rest which makes the edges of the world a wee bit smoother. 'Twill be easier for ye in the mornin'." He moved toward her again as he added, "Let's be about findin' Kiervan now."

Again Alanna shook her head. "I don't think so."

"Ye canna stay up here. My lads will do ye no harm, but Kiervan's have no respect for what ye are. And a British patrol could come upon us at any time. 'Tis not safe for ye to be remainin' topside."

She wasn't safe anywhere aboard this floating loony bin. Alanna glanced toward the rocky island in the distance. The impulse and the decision came in the same fraction of time. Without a word she spun about, grasped the railing, and vaulted over the side. In midair she righted herself and entered the water with knifelike precision.

On sale in November:

LONG AFTER MIDNIGHT
by Iris Johansen

TABOO
by Susan Johnson

STOLEN MOMENTS
by Michelle Martin